Forbidden Fruit

Luscious and Exciting Story and More Forbidden Fruit or Master Percy's Progress In and Beyond the Domestic Circle

Anonymous

i

Works of the Public Domain

ISBN-13: 978- 1974023677
ISBN-10: 1974023672

CONTENTS

PREFACE My readers of Forbidden Fruit may wish to know the origin of the work. It was this way, whilst I was staying at an out of the way village on the Sussex coast, I used to take long solitary walks, and several times saw a very beautiful girl sitting on a secluded part of the downs, attentively reading what looked like a manuscript in a black cover. Naturally I concluded she was some very studious young lady trying to improve her leisure, as she did not appear anything like the frivolous novel about what she was so intent upon.

One day, on the same foot-path, I picked up what I believed to be her manuscript book, and looking curiously at the contents, was surprised to find it was a tale of the grossest kind, scenes of love and lust depicted in the most realistic manner, with Prick, Cunt, Fuck and other things mentioned in the plainest language.

I sat down on the bank to enjoy this unexpected voluptuous treat, when suddenly I was startled by a breathless exclamation of: "That's my book! Oh, give it me back, Sir; I must have dropped it as I passed along here, a short time ago, and ran back to find it."

"Your book, Miss. I was just looking to see if there was any address in it, when I saw what it was about. Excuse my looking, it was done quite innocently, and your secret is safe with me."

Realising at once the shame of the thing, she gasped for breath, flushed crimson, and then turning pale as death, fell fainting at my feet, before I could catch her in my arms.

Reclining her against the mossy bank upon which I had been sitting, I rubbed and chafed her hands, squeezing her fingers quite painfully, in order to bring her to herself, but for several minutes without success, as there was no chance to obtain either water or brandy in such a place.

Presently she murmured "Fuck me! Shove in into me! I want it all—I must have it now;" and a succession of bawdy expressions, quite shocking from the lips of such a young girl, as she could not be more than seventeen, at most.

It was incredible she could be so depraved, but it seemed a striking confirmation of what a doctor once told me, viz, that even the most virtuous girls often use frightfully obscene words, when recovering from a fainting fit.

Anyhow, I resolved not to take advantage of her, and behave honourably to her.

As she came round a little she opened her eyes with the question: "Oh! where am I?" And catching sight of me holding her hands so tightly, all her shame returned to her in quite an overwhelming sense, and bursting into tears, she cried so bitterly, it was a long time before I could reassure her.

Promising to keep the secret of her book, I only asked one thing, and that was that she would not avoid me, and allow me to see her again.

This of course led to a close friendship between us; I lent her a variety of voluptuous books, and she let me have the manuscript to copy for my printer, but would not impart to me how she came by it, saying: "Some day, perhaps, after I am married, then I will let you Fuck me, and tell you all; it will not be long, my wedding is fixed to come off in two months time; I'm a virgin and mean to be so till I have my husband, but have to thank your forbearance that dreadful day when, you found my book, and did not take advantage of the situation. I both respect and love you for it."

She would permit me every familiarity but the one thing. We Frigged, Sucked, and enjoyed every other pleasure, both abroad, and in my own rooms, where she would visit me, having perfect liberty, living with an

2

old nurse of hers; so not a soul in the place knew anything about either of us.

When we parted it was, "Au Revoir," and some day I may have more to tell.

THE AUTHOR.

FORBIDDEN FRUIT

How well I remember my early days, almost to babyhood when it was always the care of my beautiful mother to bath me herself every day; there was also Mary my nursemaid, but when Mamma had to be away at any time the supervision of my bath was delegated to her sister. Auntie Gertie, a pretty girl of sixteen or seventeen.

Till six or seven years of age I slept in a cot in my parents' own bed-room. Papa was a very dark fine handsome man, Mamma equally so, or much more beautiful to me, had lovely golden hair and deep blue eyes full of love for me in every glance.

I can just remember one day when Mary and Auntie Gertie were giving me my bath, I thought they were looking at my little spout, as I said saucily: "What are you looking at, Papa has got such a big one."

Amongst the tricks I used to play on my nurse was one of suddenly running up to her and raising her skirts in fun, so one day when Mamma was bathing me, I suddenly said, "Mamma dear, Mary has such a lot of hair at the bottom of her belly;" making the poor girl blush crimson, as she explained my tricks to Mamma.

Another time to Auntie Gertie: "You should see my Papa hug my Mamma like a bear in bed."

After this my cot was removed to the nursery, as Master Percy was getting too observant.

What romps I used to have with Mary; then when I was about eight or nine years old, I often would insist upon sleeping with her, always creeping inside her night dress, to nestle close to her soft warm flesh.

I would kiss her titties and pretend to be a little sucking pig, as I played with her belly even as low down as the hairy part, which she always resisted my handling by keeping her own hand over it.

4

Often her motions were very curious; I fancied she was rubbing herself between her thighs, and she would finish with deep sighs and what seemed to me a tremulous shudder; generally she would also kiss me ardently.

Time passed on and I was growing quite a big boy. Somehow Mary and myself seemed instinctively to avoid ever mentioning our bed-fellow games; as far as I was concerned, there seemed something too good to be told, even to Mamma.

I must have been nearly twelve when Mary had to go home for a few days, to nurse her mother, so Auntie Gertie took her place in the nursery.

She saw me to bed about eight o'clock, and then went away, leaving me awake, wondering if she would let me get into her bed. Bye and bye I heard her enter the room, so pretending to be asleep, closed my eyes as she came to look at me, with the lamp in her hand. "What a beautiful boy, if only I dared!" I heard her say softly to herself. Then placing the lamp on a table, she came again to the bedside, and imprinted a warm kiss on my cheek, then another and another. Opening my eyes in apparent surprise, I threw my arms round her neck and gave her back kiss for kiss; this went on for quite a minute or two, till she said, laughing and blushing at the same time: "What a silly, spoony boy you are, Percy; I thought you were asleep."

"Oh, no, Auntie Gertie, dear, I do love you so, and when you kissed me I could not help paying you back; don't you love me a little?"
"Now go to sleep, there's a good boy, I must go to bed myself, put your head under the clothes, if I catch you peeping at me, I'll whip your bottom, that's all;" drawing the sheets up over my face. "Now keep like that, till the light is out."

If I could not see, my ears listened till I heard the well known ripple of her water in the chamber pot and out of shame impudence whistled, the

5

same as I had heard the groom do to Papa's horse when he wanted it to piss. Sudden darkness.

The sound of that rushing stream electrified me; sensations I had never experienced before coursed through my veins, my little pego hardened of it's own accord, so jumping out of bed, I exclaimed: "Auntie, I must give you a last kiss, how funny the noise of your pee-pee has made me feel, I am all of a tremble, just feel me," winding my arms again round her neck; she seemed only too willing to return my eager kisses, drawing me to her bosom till I could feel the firm palpitating orbs pressing against my breast.

"Come into bed, and cuddle me, Percy, I feel so chilly to night," she whispered.

Only too pleased I nestled myself by her side, still kissing and calling her my loving Auntie.

Fate had ordained I was to lose my maidenhead that night, young as I was. Her hand passed all over me, caressing every part, and she freely abandoned her bosoms to my impassioned kisses.

Presently her hand wandered down to where my stiff standing pintle was throbbing against her belly, her hand closed upon my staff, which felt to me bigger and bigger every moment, and must even then have been a good six inches.

Not a word passed between us; she glued her lips to mine, almost sucking my breath away and altogether seemed in such an agitated state, that I was nearly frightened; still I felt only too pleased, as she held my affair in her hand and slowly passed her fingers up and down, up and down, drawing back the foreskin each time. Somehow she gradually worked me into a position between her legs as we lay side by side, then she commenced rubbing the nose of my machine in a moist sort of chink embowered in the silky hair at the bottom of her stomach. One of her arms hugged me round the waist, and presently a soft whisper murmured: "Percy, push yourself close to me, it's so nice, my darling."

I followed instructions, and hand directing my instrument, it slipped in somewhere very moist and deliciously warm. She wriggled her bottom and drew me in more and more at each motion; both her hands now pushed my bottom each time in response to her forward shoves.

The game grew faster and faster; she rolled over on her back, her legs entwined over my buttocks, so as not lose the little prisoner she had got in her grot.

"Now Percy, my love, shove in hard and fast, dear, make me come, isn't it delicious, my boy?" "Oh, Auntie, you dear Auntie Gertie: where am I going to?" I ejaculated in a delirium of entrancing sensations—"Ah oh! oh!—what's going to happen, I'm bursting!" and my head fell on her shoulder as I lay nearly lifeless, all the extatic emotions of the impulsive gushes throbbing from me, as her grot seemed to grip and suck every drop of my life, so as to mingle the very essence of our being in the recesses of what I now know was her womb.

What a grip she kept on me! Something inside of her caressed the head of my instrument, and the contractions of that moist warm chink seemed to increase every moment. The folds of her adorable vagina worked up and down on my delighted pintle in a truly marvellous manner, and for the rest of my life I have never had experience of a woman so gifted as she was in that way. I was quite painfully stiff, she excited me so, and almost before I had realised all that had happened to me, the flood came again, and this time I could feel she was also gushing out love juice in response to mine; a kind of rage possessed me, I wanted to kill her by thrusting my instrument as savagely as possible, but the more I did so, the more vehement her motions became. She heaved up her bottom in desperate plunges to meet every thrust, and but for clinging very tightly round each others' waists she must have thrown me off.

Our mingled fluids spurted all over my bag of balls and flooded our thighs at every push.

At length we lay exhausted, but I was still on the top of her, and her vagina seemed as anxious to retain its working partner as before, but nature denied me the strength to go on.

"Oh, Auntie, you've killed me, it's gone dead now," as I felt it all limp and slipping away from her.

"Percy, dear, darling boy, we must go to sleep now, perhaps in the morning you will be all right again for another game. Only to think, I've taken your maidenhead, and what pleasure you have given me! Your father could not do it better."

"Has he ever put that big one of his into you there, Auntie? It must have hurt you awfully?"

"Don't call me Auntie, call me Gertie; say you love me, Percy, but never tell what we have done to-night; your Mamma doesn't mind Papa poking me, if she sees it done; we are sisters you know, and they say it is all in the family; but Mamma would be mad if she knew I had you first, so never say a word, and she won't know; but I can tell you a secret, Percy— she means to have you herself when she thinks you are old enough; but she doesn't know what a boy you are, my pet; so let me have you to myself for a little; if you do too much it will kill you; Mamma and I almost kill Papa sometimes, we want such a lot of poking, but some nice wine soon gives him strength again. He took my maidenhead to please your Mamma, who thought she would like to see it done. Ah, that did hurt: his great big engine bursting into me and stretching poor Fanny till she was all torn and bleeding. Boys are not hurt like that, it is only the poor girls who suffer when they lose their maidenhead. Take my advice, Percy, never let a girl or woman know you have ever been intimate with another; it is unkind to them, makes them jealous to think they are not the first; besides, dear boy, you don't know how delightful it was to me to think I was the first you ever put into; and only a boy, but what a boy

8

my darling Percy is!" kissing me with all the abandon of her nature. We went to sleep, but our exertions so overcame us that we were late for breakfast and had not time for a game.

"Wait till night; we shall be all the better for the delay;" she said, as we hurriedly dressed ourselves.

All that day my eyes were for my mother, and when she kissed me my heart went out to her in a manner it had never done before; the loving grace in those deep blue eyes seemed to have a new meaning for me, and her hair looked more golden than ever; was she ornamented with golden hair also at the bottom of her belly? I determined to ask Gertie about that. Auntie was three years younger than Mamma and rather slimmer in figure, but not anything so grand and adorable in my eyes; a feverish excitement pervaded my whole being, and frequently during that first eventful day when I already felt myself a man, thinking myself as good as Papa. My pego seemed to grow in importance, and raised its head, times out of number, as the thoughts of the possibility that some day I could be as free with Mamma as I now was with Auntie.

Dear Gertie could not help seeing how fascinated I was with Mamma, and once even cautioned me to watch myself or all would be found out and I should be sent to a boarding school. She herself was very careful of me, and on the sly gave me a second glass of wine at luncheon, besides helping me to the most recuperative viands on the table.

It was the same at dinner, and when at last she put me to bed at the usual time, I felt so rampageous, I made her look at my enormously distended affair.

"How rude you are Percy to night. How dare you, Sir, show that thing to me? Now, do your pee-pee at once and get into bed, or I shall whip you till your bottom is sore.

"Here is the chamber utensil. Let me see you do it properly, or goodness knows, you will wet the bed like a baby; you are so distrait."

Her laughing face and the idea of a lady holding the utensil for me, took away all power to micturate; I couldn't do it for the life of me.

"Now, go on you bad boy, don't keep me waiting all night," she said severely.

"Go away and leave off teasing me. You know I can't pee if you look at me."

She put down the pot, and almost before I even guessed what she was at, turned me over on the bed face downwards, and began smacking my bottom with all her strength.

Oh, how those spanks smarted, as she rained them on my devoted rump.

"This is for your naughtiness, Sir; will you obey me or not—Percy—is that rude thing always going to stick up and defy me like that?"

Slap—Slap—Slap—making me wince at every smack—"Oh—ah-r-re, don't
Gertie, don't that is not fun to me, you hurt me so."
"Yes, and I hope I do hurt you, you bad boy—will you—will you do as I tell you, or not—Why I declare it's as still as impudent as ever," she said, thrusting her hand beneath me to feel how I was—"there, I must serve you out!"

"Ah-r-r-re, oh, you're biting me, Gertie—oh, pray don't—pray don't bite my bottom like that, or I shall scream."

"I feel I must bite you, Percy I can't make it be good, and there's only one way to make your instrument lay down, but you must wait till I come to bed, then I will see to it, as I did last night."

This little game, and the want of sufficient rest on the previous night, made me very sleepy, and when she was gone I dropped off into a

10

beautiful slumber, and was only awakened by her kissing me. Opening my eyes, there she stood by my bedside as naked as she was born, exposing all the beauties of her figure to my enraptured gaze, but what attracted me was not the sight of the ivory globes of her swelling breast, but lower down, where the mount of Venus was shaded by a profusion of curly reddish golden hair, just beneath which I knew was concealed the warm cleft which had afforded me such infinite joy the previous night.

"Oh, Gertie let me kiss you all over, what a love you look, just like the picture of Eve in your big bible, only she has not got any hair there. Do tell me has my Mamma got the same colored hair as you, and is she like you all over?"

"Of course she has, Percy, why do you think so much of Mamma, when you have me?" she said, with quite a jealous little tone.

"What you told me about her wanting me, my own mother has made me feel so alloverish all day, your plaything has been sticking up so often, and when Mamma kissed me, I wanted her so, and you noticed it. Now I will strip too, and when you take it in that lovely place between your thighs, let me fancy it is Mamma; and I shall love you, oh, so much."

"Very well, have your own way, you funny boy; so, I'm to be nobody, and Mamma everything; never mind I shall have the pleasure," as she playfully pulled my night shirt over my head, and not being unfastened at the neck, she had me prisoner, my head and arms being confined as she pulled me off the bed.

"Now, I've got you, my boy, you can't help yourself; I'm Mamma, am I?" and in a trifle she was whipping me with something which cut and stung me dreadfully, this I afterwards found was a long thin bunch of green birch twigs she had slyly got ready for me.

I did not resist much, for every thing she did seemed only to tend to the most delightful pleasure, but I wanted to look at and enjoy the sight of

11

her charms, which was exactly what she did not intend just at the moment; she wanted to torture me and enjoy the idea of my pain and humiliation, and not to let me see the exultation shown in her face and eyes.

Her cuts made me plunge about in order to disentangle myself from the embarrassing night robe, but it took me several minutes to effect my escape, my tender buttocks suffering every moment more and more under her strokes. At length I was free, and catching her round the waist almost lifted her on to the bed, and as she was pushed back with her legs hanging over the side, and her feet still resting on the floor, I slipped down on my knees, to explore that divine spot:—"Now, Gertie, I mean to look and know all about where I was last night."

She suddenly became passive and permitted me to do as I pleased, so my explorations of the regions of love were easy.

Gently parting the abundance of reddish golden hair, I found the slightly gaping lips of her vagina bedewed with pearly drops of creamy love juice, which she must have emitted in the excitement of whipping me.

"Ah, cheat," I exclaimed. "You have given me the pain, and had the pleasure to yourself."

"Kiss me there, Percy dear, and forgive me; it was all love, as you will soon understand, I whipped you both for my own pleasure and also to make you still more ardent and fierce when shove into me."

I was an apt pupil, so parting those vermilion lips, found a little fleshly button just above the entrance I could see lower down; my fingers touched it. "There—there—that's the spot. Kiss it, you dear boy—just a little, and then make haste to push into me."

Curious to know the effect, I at once complied by sucking that little button between my lips, and also working the tip of my tongue softly over it, gently biting with my teeth now and then.

12

"Put your fingers into me, dear," she said, in a low voice, "and I shall soon come—Go on—go on—you darling love;" and just then my hand was inundated with a copious flow of her creamy essence, which so excited me, I could not wait any longer; I was ready to burst myself, so jumping up, I took one leg under each arm and rammed into her with all the strength I was capable of; my God, how she heaved to meet my attack! Her vagina seemed as stiff as my pintle, closing upon it with an extraordinary grasp, such as few women are capable of, nipping and squeezing the head of my affair each time it reached to the bottom of her womb.

We spent ourselves in a mutually copious ejaculation, and she kept heaving and wriggling, still insatiable for more, keeping me as stiff as exer, making me, boy as I was then, overflow three times before she finished me, whilst as to herself it was one continuous emission as long as I could go on pushing into her. At length we lay on the bed palpitating and breathless.

Presently she took my face between her two hands and drawing in to her lips, kissed me in the most impassioned manner.—"Percy, what a champion you are, if your Mamma did but know it; but don't be in a hurry to desert me; you will have enough of her when the time comes and even then, I don't believe she can; Papa says I'm a long way the best of the two. Now. I've smuggled a bottle of the finest Madeira up stairs, and will give my boy a couple of glasses; then we will have a new sort of, game, which you will be sure to like, and after that to sleep; we must not do too much."

I think that wine was the most invigorating I ever tasted. Unused as I was to more than a singe glass of claret at luncheon or dinner, the generous Madeira fired all the blood in my system, making me palpitate with desire to renew those love games which I had so recently learned, and still wished to know more about.

"Gertie, how kind of you to think of that. It makes me feel more of a man than ever. How stiff it is, but do give me another glass just to drink the health of your—what do you call it—you know under the hair there."

"Oh Percy, you'll be inebriated, my dear. Only this once, and if affects you much, I shall refuse a third glass another time," she said, refilling my glass.

"Now, what do you call it, Gertie? Tell me it's proper name."

"Mine," she said, slapping her hand on her lovely mount—is a C-U-N-T
(Cunt) but when girls talk together about it they call their
"Fanny"—but I like the word Cunt—always call it that, Percy, when alone with me—and, your's, dear, what do boys their affairs?"
"You know I have never been to school and have been so much at home with Mamma, you, and Mary, that I hardly know the right name for my thing; but what does Papa call his?"

"Papa calls it his Prick—Mamma calls it a glorious Cock—and I, I use either name. Here Percy, we will drink to Cock and Cunt, and may they never get tired of love; a stiff Standing Prick, and a Cunt ready for it."
We emptied our glasses and she placed them on the table, then getting on the bed, stretched herself by my side, and kissed me ardently, darting her velvety tongue between my lips, till I could endure it no longer, and wanted to mount up as before.

"No, not that way this time, we will try a new pleasure; I want to taste and swallow the very essence of your being."

Reversing herself upside down by my side, and taking my stiff machine in her mouth, began to suck and roll her tongue round its head, in the most delicious manner. At the same time she pressed her mount against my face, as a challenge for me to reciprocate her attentions to my prick. Words were not required. I knew instinctively what I ought to do, so my

14

fingers parted the lips of her luscious Cunt, and my tongue was at once busy about La Rose d'Amour, the little spot where the slightest titillations of a tongue will arouse even in the coldest temperament the most ardent sensations of desire, and at once dispel any ideas of resistance to the due course of pleasure.

It is the real touch-hole, which once fired, lets off all the pent up sources of voluptuousness; let the chilly virgin be but once assaulted there by finger or tongue, and she is lost; Shame—Prudence—every thought, save of utter abandonment—all vanish as the conquering hero pursues his advantage;—and it is the same with a boy who for the first time finds pintle between the lips of an ardent girl who is all-a-fire to enjoy his youthful virility.

Each one abandons every charm to the other; desire to do courses hotly through their veins, each seems anxious to devour the other; so it was with us, she flooded my mouth at the same instant as I felt my very life melting away and spurting down her eager throat.

Not a drop of the creamy emission escaped me; I was sucking her life, her soul, and wanted more each moment. This game lasted a considerable time. After each spend, our lips still kept possession of the organ of love, sucking and playing our tongues in the most lascivious way we could imagine to prolong and bring on the exotic spasms again and again.

Exhausted at length, we settled ourselves to sleep, with a mutual kiss and thanks for the delicious pleasures afforded.

Beautiful dreams haunted my sleeping hours and still more inflamed my now thoroughly awakened manhood. Recently I had read the mythological tale of the three goddesses, Juno, Venus and Minerva appealing to the shepherd Paris for the prize of the golden apple; as drapery was very rare in those Pagan days, no doubt they stood before him in all the glories of their matchless beauty.

15

Visions of my glorious golden haired Mamma, Auntie Gertie, and Mary, standing before me, as if I had to chose which was most desirable; the last named a swarthy beauty of twenty, with small figure, but a model of gracefulness, seemed indeed to challenge comparison with my two lovely relatives, and much as I longed to possess Mamma, this vision of Mary made a very lasting impression on my mind; beyond them stretching away in the dim perspective were quite a procession of attendant houris, all sizes, ages, and styles of complexion and beauty from very little ones to the fat, fair, and forty. Was this prophetic of my future career amongst the fair sex, viz, beginning at home with the first principal figures, and then to revel in a succession of loveliness for a long time to come; as I opened my eyes, that was the thought which came to me, and I resolved to have sweet swarthy Mary as soon as she returned to her duties; it should be "Nolens Votens;" I was strong enough to make her let me have my way.

My instrument, inflamed by both dream and resolves, stood rampant, and attracted Gertie's attention as she opened her eyes:

"My Goodness, Percy, what an erection!—I have just been dreaming of you pushing into your Mamma on the sofa, whilst I sat astraddle of Papa on his Cock, and rode up and down, as you pleased your mother; how I should have liked it to be real; perhaps it will some day—put your hand down and feel how wet I am, it made me come in a flood—and now you are almost as bad—have you been dreaming too?"

I confessed as much with respect to her and Mamma, but kept Mary to myself for fear Auntie might spoil my anticipated pleasure in that quarter.

"It's getting late, my boy, so let me have it quick, just the same as I was dreaming I was on your Papa—riding on your dear Cock."

I was already on my back, as she placed herself across me kneeling on her knees, and so taking Mr. Pego in one hand, she directed his head to the well lubricated slit so ready to take him in, gently impaling herself as

16

her body gradually pressed down on my inflamed Prick. The long slow insertion into that furnace of love was delicious, and as she felt the head at last reach the very entrance to her longing womb, her sperm came in a flood. Mine also had been so put up that the spasmodic contractions of the folds of the innermost parts of her vagina at the moments of emission drew an equally copious ejaculation from me.

"My God, Percy, that will make a baby, I must syringe at once!" she said, as soon as she recovered herself and finished kissing me. "What exquisite pleasure! We ought to go on, but I must not run the risk;" and springing off me, in spite of my efforts to detain her in my arms, she proceeded to syringe herself most effectually with an enema, using a very slight solution of sulfate of zinc, which will always prevent impregnation if done quickly after coition. As she explained to me, the critical moment such as we had just experienced only happened now and then, but that the female had such a very peculiar sensation, she could not possibly mistake it, and only a careless girl, or one who really wished for a child, would neglect to syringe the moment it was all over.

Gertie had me to herself for some days, before Mary returned, but my vision had never lost its effects on my mind.

Auntie was very reluctant to give up her charge, but there was no available excuse. She admonished me to be very circumspect and we would enjoy ourselves every possible chance. "Some night," she whispered, "you can steal into my room when Mary is asleep, but don't let her know anything, or you will be sent away, my love."

The short time that Mary had been away, seemed to have worked quite a change in her manner towards me, she seemed to have grown suddenly shy and reserved, and the first night even neglected to give me the usual conventional kiss, and when she retired herself, was very careful to put out the light before doing certain little things.

"All right, my beauty," I thought to myself. One good night's rest, then for an explanation or else something better.

17

She was restless, and as I lay awake, thinking over all my game with Auntie Gertie, Mary was tossing about and unsettled. I could hardly restrain myself from jumping up and getting into her bed.

At length her heavy breathing told me she slept, but evidently dreaming, as I could hear little words now and then, such as: "Don't Georges— you shan't—indeed you shan't—I'll slap your face if you go on so."

Sleep overcame me at last, and when I opened my eyes in the morning she had left the room. All day my eyes feasted on Mamma and I could see Gertie pouting with vexation at my evident desire for the maternal connexion. This served my purpose exactly, as it took away all suspicion of my design upon Mary.

"Don't look at Mamma like that, Percy, or I shall begin to dislike you, my boy, and shan't let you love me again," she whispered, when she got me alone.

"Oh, there's no harm in looking. Gertie, you know you told me she meant to have me, when I am old enough, and I'll let her know that some day before very long."

"You tease. I'll whip your bottom, when I get you alone, you bad boy; you only want to make me jealous."

"Then don't be so silly Gertie. Looking at Mamma does no harm yet, but
I do so want to kiss her Cunt."
"Fie, for shame, sir! Be off and behave yourself."

That day seemed a very long one to me, but bed time came as last. Mary was retiring as on the previous evening, but I waited till she had put out the light, and got into bed.

"Mary," I said, "why don't you kiss me since you come back?"

"Oh! Master Percy, you are such a big boy now, we ought to leave off that," was the reply.

"But what is the harm; we always did, and used to have such nice games together; shall I come and kiss you just now?"

"No, no, I won't allow it any more, besides—besides."

"Besides, what?" I said, getting out, and going to her bedside: "Besides, I mean to kiss you and will make you kiss me." "Go away! Percy, you shan't!" as she covered her head with the bed-clothes.

"That's better than Master Percy; now, I will kiss you, Mary dear, so don't make a fuss, but kiss me back."

"Well, just once, then go back to bed," she said, raising her head.

"There's a dear girl," I replied kissing her on the lips; "Kiss me back or I'll pull the clothes off and slap you."

Her lips returned my osculation and I tried to slip the tip of my tongue into her mouth as I prevented her taking her face away, and sucked in her very breath till she seemed to quiver all over, and her lip relaxed a little till the tips of our tongues fairly met.

This dalliance continued for some minutes till one of my hands found its way inside her night chemise, and grabbed the heaving globes of her bosom, moulding them and playing with the saucy nipples which stuck up as firm as my Cock, which was in a fiery state of expectation.

"Now, go away do, you impudent boy, where have you learnt such tricks, Percy?" she whispered as she faintly attempted to push me away.

19

"Nowhere, only I do so like to feel and kiss you, Mary, you are so warm and soft, and kiss so nicely my dear;" as I was gently sliding into the bed beside her.

"What makes you like kissing so? Don't Mamma or auntie Gertie kiss you enough, you silly boy."

"Oh, but that's different, I can't feel them all over, as I do you; as I hugged my body close to hers, those palpitating bosoms now beating against my breast."

"How queer you make me feel, Mary. Don't you notice my affair stiff and hard against you belly; let us lay close to each other, and your warm flesh against mine," pulling up her chemise to her waist.

"How is it you have hair there, dear, and I have none about mine!" My hand was groping to get a finger in her slit, and if possible to touch the spot I knew so well.

"No, Percy, you mustn't put your hand there, that thing of yours is hard against my belly. Put it away do."

"Between your legs, Mary, I seem to feel sure that is the place; let me lay between your legs and rub my belly against yours; how hot you are there!" Both my hands were trying to force open her thighs, which she kept firmly closed.

"You shan't—you shan't, you bad boy, what do you mean by such goings on, Percy?"

A sudden frenzy impelled me to exert all my strength; little by little, I got one leg between hers, as I pushed her over on her back.—"I will," I said, grinding my teeth in desperation; "You shall let me, Mary; now, don't fight so, it's no use."
We struggled on in silence, she was almost a strong as myself, but panting for breath she was gradually mastered by my dogged resolve to

20

win my way:—"Oh, oh, you shan't, indeed you shan't;" as I got a finger fairly in her slit, which was quite moist and slimy, as no doubt the ardour of our struggles had brought on an emission.

The head of my Cock at last got lodged just inside the moist lips of her vulva; she gave a tremulous shudder, and I thought the victory was won, but with quite sudden desperation, she rolled herself almost on her side, but I clasped one arm firmly round her waist, and the other hand gave her buttocks such a savage pinch, that with a sharp "Oh! oh!" her bottom heaved up a little, and I felt my champion gain a little way in; again she struggled desperately, and actually bit my shoulder, but that only made me more savage.

Slowly I pushed up to her last virgin defence. "You shan't, Oh Percy, you'll ruin me, do get away; you'll kill me.—Oh—Ah-r-r-re!" as struggling and wriggling to resist me, her motions actually helped to accomplish the rape, for thrusting fiercely just as she heaved a little to throw me off, the hymen was broken, and my Cock triumphed over that stubbornly contested virginity.

So ignorant was I of the ethics of copulation that I had no idea of the irreparable damage I had done to poor Mary.

"There, I told you I would, you couldn't prevent me getting into you, my dear, and how lovely it feels now I am there; my Cock is inside you, and your Cunt holds, it so delightfully tight". I kissed her again and again, and began to move by instrument inside her, but she only responded by heartbroken sobs, and her face was wet with tears.

"What is the matter dear, don't you like it; what a struggle we had, but that only added to the fun of the thing; have I indeed hurt you so much? Cheer up and join in the game now."

"Ah, Percy," she sobbed, "you have robbed me of the only jewel I possessed; I can never get married now, any one could know some one

21

had broken through my hymen;" and she sobbed bitterly, so much so, that I was really distressed, and ashamed of my violence.

"Oh! what have I done? Do tell me Mary, don't cry so, dry up your tears, you know I love you."

"And so I do you Percy, my own boy; and, oh, I was so afraid it would happen some day. Now, kiss me and tell me truly, who taught you to be so rude; you must have had a lesson from your Auntie Gertie whilst I was away. I know what she is, so hot, so lustful; she wants every man and boy she can get; I know your Papa pokes her, and so does your cousin Mr. Shore, and even when she goes out for a ride with our groom Parsons, or a walk by herself, she takes a small syringe and a bottle of lotion in her pocket, in case of accident, but I know what sort of accident she means. Now, tell me, and I'll keep your secret: but never let her suspect I know, or I should lose my place. Now, Percy, I'm sure she taught you. Tell me truly, dear."

Certain that I could not hide the truth from the dear girl, I confessed as to my aunt, but nothing more. "Mary dear," I said, "we will keep our secret to ourselves, she will never suspect you."

"Oh, you little love, you shall be all mine; that cat, beautiful as she is, shan't have you," she said, squeezing me in her arms, and kissing me rapturously.—"All mine, and I feel it throbbing inside of me, Percy, push again now, gently at first, as I feel rather sore, perhaps it will soon get easier. Ah, that's it, how nice, draw out nearly, and then in again softly, dear; that's it, how, lovely! Oh! what is that shooting into me, like a spurt of hot balm, right up to my heart?—Oh! Oh! I'm coming too!" she sobbed in ecstasy—"what divine pleasure—how you pushed at that moment—go on, dear, don't stop, it's too ravishing to waste a moment!" as she instinctively entwined her legs over me, and wriggled her bottom in excess of pleasure, as our love juices mingled in her womb; then at last she stretched herself out at length, her Cunt closely nipping Cupid's battering ram, her arms tightly holding me almost like a vice, her lips played with mine in long kisses, our tongues darting into each other's

22

mouths in the most luscious manner, all the while the inner folds of her tight fitting sheath kept me prisoner, and treated my Cock to the most delicious contractions and pressures, till I was so inflamed, Cupid's charger plunged on his mad career once more, making my dark beauty writhe and squirm in the excess of her ecstatic emotion; several times we seemed to stop by mutual consent, and lay for a while enjoying those heavenly sensations. After thus delaying the final crisis to the uttermost, the moment came when the life flood could no longer be kept back, and our simultaneous emission drowned the organs of love so profusely that our thighs were deluged as we continued to churn in the creamy overflow.

This finished our game for the night, and when my eyes opened in the morning she lay naked by my side, having thrown off her blood-stained chemise. She was awake. "Ah! Percy, my love, I thought you would never wake, but I did not like to touch you: see what a mess the bed is in—it was a real rape—you would never have done it if I had been strong enough—But now, oh, how I love my boy!"

The sight that met my eyes did indeed give evidence of something awful—blood stains—patches of dried semen, discoloured by blood.

"My God, Mary, what will you do? We shall be found out."

"Kiss you for it, Percy. Don't be afraid, I will change the sheets and make it right," gluing her lips to mine, as if she would suck my breath away, whilst one of her hands found out my now standing champion ready for the fray.

"Let me have it again, dear, before I get up; I want you so much."

"Well then, Mary my love, try Auntie Gertie's plan; kneel across me and help yourself, whilst I lay on my back and enjoy the sight of your beautiful body as you ride up and down on my Cock; oh, I do think a dark girl like you beats all fair beauties."

"What a flatterer to say that, you artful boy—when you know, and have seen such a beauty as your aunt," as she slowly impaled herself on my rampant engine. "Did she teach you that way? Well she knows what's good any how—Ar-r-re—it's up so far, let me sit and feel it like that for a moment."

With sparkling eyes and a smile on her lips which parted just enough to show me a row of pearls of the whitest ivory, and so perfect that being bitten by them could only be a pleasure. Then again the contrast between this dark olive tinted Venus and the creamy colored complexion of my aunt with her reddish-golden haired mount and the black silky down which ornamented the tight fitting sheath, which now was enjoying possession of my Cock. All these so tired my imagination, that I heaved up my buttocks to start another heat in love's steeple chase, and the little dark tilly at once bounded on her course with all the fire of her nature.

"Ah," she said, slackening the pace, "it is too good to hurry like that," and she laid herself full length over my body, devouring my mouth with her hot tonguing kisses, whilst her Cunt kept possession of my Prick, and treated it to a course of the most exquisite compressions imaginable, till at length she suddenly resumed the proper position and riding furiously for a moment or two, fell exhausted on my bosom as gushes of spend flooded my delighted Cock and invited it to shoot its essence into her very vitals.

"Ah," she said, as at last she reluctantly dressed herself; "what a man you will make, and what a lot of girls you will want. Poor me will be nowhere, but you shall always have me, when you want a bit of my black Fanny— Black for Beauty—you know; much as you may sometimes run after the fair ones."

Mary and I indulged in every variety of voluptuous pleasures; we needed no further instruction, but tried everything we could think of, even to pissing in each other's mouths, as a finale after a long bout of erotic excitements.

24

She had the prettiest of underclothing and one of my delights was to be dressed up as a girl, in chemise, drawers and corset; then she would put on my shirt and trousers, and in this kind of demi-toilette we had many a spree in our bedroom, and she did look a pretty boy. She would kiss and chuck me under the chin, calling me her pretty Jemima—"Pretty Jemima, don't say no, what a nice soft Fanny you have, my dear;" as she would put her hands under my chemise and gently wag Mr. Peaslin, who was always in a state of erection. Perhaps it was the aroma of her chemise and drawers which had such a magnetic effect on me, always bringing on a violent priapism. She would push me back on the edge of the bed, and opening her trousers, pretend to get into me, and of course I slipped into her; this was quite a fancy of hers. She would say: "Jemima darling, how deliciously you squeeze my Prick! Do I please you, darling? Am I fucking you nicely?"

For in a very short time we got to relish all the expressions so piquant in bawdy language and which give such a zest to the fullest enjoyment. When sometimes I would say to her: "I mean to give you a beautiful Fuck," she would exclaim: "Say that again. I like to hear you say that;" and as to our masquerading in each other's clothes, she said it made her feel a double pleasure when my Prick was so tight inside her, it seemed to be part of herself and it really appeared as if she was Fucking me, as I lay beneath her, on the edge of the bed; "imagination is everything, my dear, when you can have your Aunt, or any girl you fancy, even your own Mother, if you think of her as you Fuck me."

When she talked like this, "Did she know anything?" I thought to myself; so one night I said: "Mary dear, do you think Mamma is fond of Fucking, and does Papa do enough for her? What do you think?"

"I don't believe one single man would satisfy your Mother or your aunt; I will tell you a great secret of something I once saw, which so upset me at the time, that I rally think if a nice young man had been there, my maidenhead would never have been left for you."

25

The summer before last, you will remember Capt. Devereux your uncle, and who of course is brother to both your mother and your aunt, stayed here for a week, before he went to India, where he is now; he tried to be very familiar with me, but I was too shy and ran away when he tried to give me a kiss.

You know your mother's boudoir is only separated from this room by the big closet between, which is used for hanging up dresses, as that is so much better than having them folded. You know what a roomy place it is, with a long row of pegs on one side, and the big linen press at the end; besides the door into the corridor, there is one into the boudoir, half glass covered with a pink silk blind.

Well, one day I was in there taking out the dresses, to keep them free of moth when I heard the key turned in the lock of the door into the corridor, and your mother's voice: "No one can go in there now, and we can't be disturbed," as the Captain and his two sisters entered the boudoir. I don't know why I didn't knock to be let out at once, but when I thought of doing so, I heard the Captain's voice:—I suppose, Selina, you must be first. I want a Fuck awfully bad; we've got the whole morning to ourselves, so there is plenty of time for Gert; and my dear sisters, how we shall miss each other when I can never visit you. It's an awful bore being sent out to India, but I suppose there will be game amongst the officers' wives and daughters; our Colonel takes out all his family and has two or three fizzing girls who will soon ripen in the Indian sun.

"Oh, Horace," exclaimed your Mother. "I never had such a fucker as you, and you taught me and Gert all we know in the Art of Love. Come to my arms, my brother, the more wicked it is to be Fucked by you, the more piquant is our enjoyment:—Take it out, Gert, and put it into me, I will do as much for you presently, and lick him up too, if I make him too limp."

You may be sure I could not resist a peep, and at once thought of Solomon's proverb about the "Wonderful way of a man with a Maid," and now was a chance to learn something. So kneeling behind the glass door, I slipped a little corner of the blind aside and what did I see? Your own Mother leaning forward over the scroll end of the couch, with her dress and skirts all turned up over her back; she had on black silk knickers trimmed with a golden fringe, and light pink silk chemise and stockings; the Captain was opening her drawers and putting the tail of the chemise aside, whilst your aunt was busy unbuttoning his trousers and taking out "Oh, such a big beautiful Prick," quite nine or ten inches long, which she presented to your Mother's bottom, and I really thought he was going to push it into the wrong place, but his sister directed it lower down, and I could just see the lovely fleshy lips of your Mother's Cunt, as it fairly sucked him in, she pushing out her bottom in the rudest possible way, to meet his advance.

His shaft was as white as ivory ornamented at its base by reddish brown hair, and as his hands took a firm grip of her buttocks, drawing them towards him every time he pushed home, and I could see each movement, it was a sight to impress a girl like myself, who had never yet surrendered to a man. Ravishing indeed to watch the amorous play of your Mother's splendid Cunt, as he worked in and out, withdrawing till he nearly exposed the inflamed head of his Prick, then plunging in again to her apparent delight.

The black silk showing off the white skin to perfection, but what impressed me most as I watched the piston-like action of the Captain's affair, was to see how the fleshy lips of her Fanny clung to it each time it withdrew. I could hear quite an audible sucking sound, and those lips gradually deepened in colour from their original fleshy tint, till at the apex of excitement they were quite a splendid vermilion hue; then came the emission, which must have been copious as it spurted out in thick creamy and frothy jets, as he continued to work on.

"Horace—Horace—let me have it, balls and all—spunk into me now!" your Mother almost shrieked in her frenzy.

"Now! Now! Selina, I'm coming—I'm bursting my love—Oh, Gert, work your fingers well," was his response, whilst your aunt was doing all she could to increase his ardour by working her fingers in his bottom-hole.

I was almost frantic myself at such a sight. My hand could not but seek my own gap, and quite unconsciously rubbed and frigged myself, whilst I feel sure my eyes must have been starting from their sockets, so intensely was I fascinated by the incestuous scene enacted before me. Within a few minutes they ran another course, and came again with cries of pleasures and bawdy expressions.

The Captain now withdrew, his machine hanging down looked quite crestfallen and limp, covered with glistening spend which dripped off on to the floor; your Mother retained her position, as if too tired to get up, when to my surprise your aunt Gert, proceeded to kiss and suck her sister's reeking Cunt which was still all of a quiver, those now vermilion lips twitching as if still anxious for more.

Pushing the thighs as wide apart as possible, your aunt buried her face between those luxurious buttocks, and seemed eager to secure every drop of the precious elixir that was slowly oozing out. "Oh, how lovely!" your mother said, with a sigh of pleasure; "Come to me Horace, let me revive the drooping courage of your glorious Prick; whose lips but mine ought to raise it again for dear Gert? What intense felicity you gave me, my dear?" as he placed himself kneeling on the couch so as to bring his affair into position for her to take it into her mouth, which she did with great avidity, her hands gently holding back the foreskin and caressing his hairy balls, as first giving a good suck in her mouth she proceeded to titillate the little orifice in its head with the tip of her velvety tongue. The effect was marvellous to me. The before limp affair almost jumped into life again by a series of jerks till it stood even more proudly than ever. How she fondled that resuscitated Cock and handled his balls till his eyes started with lust, and his bottom wriggled as if he would soon be brought to the spending point again.

"No, no, I won't make you come Horace. Let Gert have her due, she's a dear girl, and never jealous of me, are you Gert? So I let her be as much Fred's wife as I am, and we three have some rare razzle-dazzles, I can tell you, same as we do with you."

Selina, your Mother, now made Gert lay on her back on the couch, and inserting her brother's Prick in the beautiful Cunt you know so well, "There, dears, go on and I will do all I can to add to your pleasure;" saying which, she pulled Horace's trousers down to his heels, and turning his shirt tail well up, handled his balls from behind for a few moments:

"Ah, you Fucker," she exclaimed, "you like Gert better than me, but no matter—there—there—there—there—go on and Fuck her. Spend into her!" giving four tremendous slaps with her hand, which made him fairly wince.

Then as if suddenly remembering something, she opened a long box ottoman, and took out a bunch of birch twigs, elegantly tied up with ribbons, with which she proceeded to attack his firm looking fleshy rump.

"Lay on Selina, don't spare me, drive me well," said the Captain.
"That's just what is wanted."
This excited my imagination to the utmost; how could a whipping add to his enjoyment. Selina did not keep me waiting long, she touched him up smartly, giving light stinging strokes, at least I feel certain they must have been stingers, to judge from the lovely rosy tint she soon raised on those firm white buttocks of his, which gradually quivered more and more as he worked rapidly in your aunt's pretty Cunt; I could see his white shaft almost withdrawn, to be plunged in again with ever increasing verve. The more Selina whipped and made his bottom smart the more furiously he Fucked her.

Presently your Mother shifted her position, so as to cut towards the division of his bottom, and make the tips of the pliant birch even reach the jewel bag, which was about to shoot its balm of love into her sister.

Gert was almost mad with lust; she fairly squealed: "Fuck faster, you dear brother, let me feel it well up at every stroke—Oh, I must come now, Eeecch?—what a gust—what a man to poke—my love, I'm spending—oh, Heavens—How delicious!"

After a short rest, laying soaking his tool in that flood of mixed love juice, he was going to withdraw, but Selina interposed.

"Gee up—Gee up—you haven't half done your duty yet, Sir; hold him tight, Gert, and I'll soon make him start and keep up to it properly."

Your aunt clasped him tightly in her arms, renewing her kisses on his lips, darting her tongue into his mouth; then finding he returned her kisses and did not attempt to get away, one hand stole down to his now languid Prick, and began to Frig it, keeping the head still within the lips of her inflamed Cunt, whilst your Mother began to lecture him.

"So, Sir, you don't want to go on Fucking my sister, when you owe her so much pleasure, but I'll see you don't defraud her of what is fairly due;—will you move Sir, or, must I scalp your bottom, for you, eh?"

"You're used up and languid, are you? I believe you will go to sleep on the top of Gert—there—there—move will you!" giving a couple of very vicious cuts, which left a lot of long fiery marks across his bottom.

"Oh, Selina don't, you hurt so, let me rest a minute or two."

"No, Sir, no; got on this minute. Gert, take that thing out of you, and show me how it is—what a limp, lazy, done-up looking thing;" as the Captain, raising himself a little off Gert, gave a chance to your Mother, who at once smartly switched her birch about the ruddy head of

Mr. Coocks, as your aunt exposed with the foreskin drawn back. "Ah-r-r-r-re, Oh! I can't stand that Selina; you are cruel."

"Cruel—then put it back into Gert's Cunt, and I will whip your backside well, till you do Fuck her properly, Sir."

Saying which, she pressed him down on her sister, who put the smarting head into her nest to soothe it and your Mother keeping her left hand on the middle of his back, went on whisking the twigs in every direction across his buttocks, till the red smacks showed all over the surface, and little drops of blood oozed from the excoriated skim; I could see he winced under her severity, but his Prick swelled visibly at every stroke, and Gert heaved up to meet each thrust, as he plunged on with erotic fury, throwing her pretty stockinged legs over his loins, giving me a splendid view of her luscious Cunt as the vermilion lips clung round the white shaft of his tool; there seemed to be such a lot of sperm mixed up in her vagina that in spite of the sound of the birching which your Mother kept up regardless, of which bottom had the benefit of it, I could hear sloppy noise each time his affair plunged up to the hilt in that well lubricated receptacle, the frothy creamy looking spend hanging in patches about the hair which embellished their parts, running over his balls, and trickling in quite a rill between the parting of her thighs.

At length Selina dropped the rod, and kneeling behind them used both her hands to tickle his balls and Frig his Prick, holding back the foreskin in a way that must have been almost painful as she seemed to drag it backwards, then suddenly letting his Prick go as she felt the crisis coming, rammed a couple of her well oiled fingers up his bottom-hole and Frigged him there, exclaiming: "Horace, well done, I felt the bursting throb. Wasn't it splendid Gert, dear?"

Both Fuckers seemed thoroughly exhausted when their crisis of ecstasy and endearments ceased, but your Mother kept her fingers going for a little till thoroughly assured they had spent the last drop and could no more.

31

After this she produced a bottle of some liqueur which seemed to have a revivifying effect upon all three, for the sisters stripped every rag off their brother and reduced their own clothing till they stood in nothing but chemise, drawers, stockings and their pretty boots.

"You like to see us like this Horace," said Selina, the two standing before him. He sat on the couch, lifting their pouting Cunts from the openings in the black silk drawers, his Prick standing again as if it had not had the least satisfaction.

"Come on, girls, for a wind up. Selina shall be St. George, as I lay back on the couch and suck Gert's delicious Cunt."

All were so voluptuously wound up, they got into position at once, the two beautiful sisters embracing and tongue kissing each other as they rode, the one on the Prick and the other over the sucking mouth of their brother. Gert and Selina seemed ready to devour each other with their lustful kisses, and when apparently they had both come more than once they changed places upon their recumbent brother; all finished with a chorus of bawdy words, sighs, and cries expressing the agony of their delight.

You may be sure I was glad when at last it was all over, and they went to their rooms to rest awhile before luncheon, which allowed me to escape from my awkward position in an awful state of amorous excitement which quite demoralised me, but I never trusted myself to spy on them again, although I know each day the Captain remained they retired to your Mother's boudoir. It was indeed a lesson to me in the philosophy of the sexes.

"But you don't think Mamma is ever likely to take liberties with me, do you?"

"I don't know so much about that; every one fancies young people, even myself, dear; I think you are far more delicious to enjoy than any big man could possibly be; and—and—but I will tell you; my own father

32

when I was lately at home, tried all he could to seduce me, going as far as to let me see his big standing affair one Sunday when I entered the room as he was reading the weekly paper, and I suppose had been Frigging himself; he had some excuse for that, as Mother was too ill to let him have what he wanted; but he quite frightened me, as I entered the room, by suddenly lifting the newspaper from before him, and letting me see his tremendous thing with its fiery red head; of course I rushed out of the room, but in an hour or two, when I was laying the supper table, he took me on his knee and tried to put a hand under my clothes, at the same time kissing me and shoving his tongue between my lips. 'Father, Father, for shame, I'll scream if you don't let me go!' was all I could say, as I struggled to prevent his hand getting between my thighs, and I suppose he was frightened as he allowed me to get away. This made me think over things, and be very distant to you when I came back; so you can guess, if my good old Father wanted me, your Mamma may be equally taken with you, especially any time Papa is away and she feels the want of him.

Now Percy, comfort Fanny a bit; you don't know how randy she feels, put your hand on her, dear, just play with the little button, as we have one of our delicious tongue kisses."

I did all I could to oblige her, with my fingers, my tremendously swollen Prick pressing all the while against her mount and frigging himself by rubbing his nose in the hairy moss of her mount. This could not last long. She opened her thighs and, drawing me upon her, directed my eager tool to her burning slit.

I pushed in slowly, enjoying the gradual insertion, till its head was gently taken in charge by the nippers, which she had in such perfection; it seemed to me just like a baby hand pressing and caressing my delighted instrument, and we enjoyed this sort of dalliance for some minutes; neither spoke, but our lips and tongues eloquently proved the intensity of our feelings. At length she suddenly bucked up her bottom, as a challenge to me go on. Thus spurred on, I slowly drew out to the very head of my Prick, then gently pushing in again, kept repeating the motion, each time gradually increasing the pace, till we arrived at the short digs, when clinging closely to her, my hands pressed up her bottom till we could scarcely move, as the spurts of our semen mingled in her womb, and I felt her receive it with the same peculiar and perceptible shudder of delight which warned my aunt to use her syringe at once.

"Oh, Mary, I've done it for you; that will make a baby the image of myself."

"Not if I can prevent it, Percy, the very last time I went to the chemist's I bought an enema and some sulphate of zinc, so you will see I don't want any babies; if you only knew what an awful thing it is for an unmarried girl to have one, you would not wish to have it happen to me."

She jumped up and syringed herself at once, as carefully as my aunt had done.

It is impossible to relate all our sprees, but I had to please Auntie now and then, when she got a chance. And so six months rolled away, and I was growing rapidly; my especial delight was to contemplate the development of my Prick, which seemed to improve daily, and must have grown to quite eight inches, being thick in proportion; I believe it was the thorough and regular irrigation by Mary's spendings which brought on such perfection. The more it grew, the more my desire for my Mother increased, which of course I kept to myself, when one day Papa had to go off almost without notice to America about a property he had over there. Mamma and Gert both cried a good bit when he started, but I asked him to bring me home a nice present.—"Some diamonds will do, Papa," I said kissing him. "What a silly innocent boy you are, Percy; they are cheaper here and your Mamma and Gert would like a lot first, when I have money enough; you shall have a necklace of grizzlybear's claws, and we'll dress you up as a girl; won't it be fun, Selina? There—there, my boy. I won't forget you;" giving me a last kiss, and then embracing Gert and Mamma, in long luscious kisses, saying: "Cheer up, don't cry," as he jumped into the carriage and drove off.

34

I cheered up immensely, as his absence would be my opportunity, and that very night, in Mary's arms, I enjoyed my Mamma in imagination. Several days passed, but one morning early my Auntie Gertie started for a long day's picnic with some friends, and took Mary to attend upon her.

Mamma took her breakfast in bed, so I went to say good-morning and kiss her; she was asleep and I had a grand view of her really magnificent bosom, as being very warm weather, she had on only a low necked chemise; how long I stood to admire the snowy whiteness of the large full bosoms as they rose and feel under my ardent gaze at each respiration, and I was going to awaken her by kissing them, when a sudden idea pleased me better; going to the drawers where I knew she kept her under clothing, I selected a pink silk chemise, and was about to take a pair of black silk drawers, only my eyes lighted upon some open net-work tights of dark blue silk, a pair of golden garters, lovely blue silk hose and a pretty pair of Turkish slippers, which looked just made for my small feet; looking in the wardrobe I spied a duck of a dressing gown, of almost transparent white muslin, which would show the figure inside and display the most attractive charms.

Running away to the nursery on the next corridor, I soon put off my own things, arrayed myself in the feminine attire, and, looking in the glass opened the dressing gown and lifted up my chemise to see how I looked beneath. Neither my Mamma or my Aunt were big women; they were rather what I call the thoroughbred type, about the Venus height and slim, with splendid bottoms which I know must have been cultivated by the most careful corsetage from earliest girlhood, so being a well grown boy, the things just suited me. But to return to the looking-glass, it made me in love with myself; the pretty stockings, legs, garters and slippers, but what almost took my breath away was the sight of the blue open network tights, which my ample thighs filled up so that they fitted me to perfection, the blue showing up the flesh tint beneath in a most ravishing manner and my Cock actually began to stand as I contemplated the sight of myself, and thought of the effect it might have on my Mamma. I felt so wicked, and as I passed along the corridor—

"La, what a pretty girl you make, Master Percy," came from a pretty young chamber maid, as I passed her. "Do you think so, Patty," I replied, "Just look at my chemise and how I am dressed underneath," opening my robe to give her a view. I felt so full of devilry that I was half inclined to pull her into the nursery for a game.

"My Goodness!" she exclaimed, in surprise, "tights and all, you don't look quite comfortable, but you'll do;" as her eyes must have caught sight of my state of erection. "See what your Mamma will think of you," with a curious look on her face.

"Kiss me then, Patty," I said giving her a hug and pressing my lips to hers, which she freely returned. "Now, go along and don't be rude, Mary must have taught you something."

"Could you teach me anything, Patty, will you give me a lesson some day?" I said, looking full in her eyes; "I think you can."

Blushing crimson, the girl got away from me, and ran into one of the rooms; perhaps she expected to be followed, but I had other games in view, relegating the pretty Patty to some future opportunity.

Entering Mamma's bed room as quietly as possible, I again contemplated that divine bust till my Prick was rampantly stiff, the compression of the net-work tights seeming only to increase the lascivious desire which inflamed it more and more every moment. I was hot all over, and my trepidation was so great, my knees knocked together; a shiver passed through my frame.

Dare I kiss them? How awful should I be repulsed. Desperation gave me courage.

"My beautiful Mamma, do let me kiss your lovely titties?" was all I could say almost in a whisper as my voice quite failed, so great was my agitation. First laying my burning cheek by the side of her heaving bosom, I took a nipple between my lips, but had hardly done so, when:

36

"My darling boy, are you kissing your Mother's bosom? I was just dreaming of my Percy. How nice of you to awake me like that;" but seeing my get up, she started in surprise: "What have you got on? my things, oh, you funny boy!" drawing my face to hers, and giving me such kisses as I had never had from her before; they were like flames, making my blood boil in a moment.

"Now, let me see how you have dressed your self, Percy," opening the muslin robe. "Ah, chemise too, none of your own things." Playfully lifting it up, you should have seen her eyes start as she caught sight of my lower parts encased in her own open-net, blue tights; seeing how Mr. John Thomas was excited, and seemed fit to break out at the instant.

"They are not big enough, they irritate you, Percy let me get them off," she said, raising herself and as the bed-clothes fell back giving me a sight of her golden-haired mount for a moment quickly as she pushed her chemise over it. It was perfectly maddening, but I had to act the innocent, and know nothing. "Come on the bed, then I can pull them off, you silly boy, why did you put them on?" So I mounted on the bed by her side, and she assisted me to remove the tights, lingering, as I thought, unnecessarily long in doing so.

"Now, I can cuddle my boy. I haven't had you to myself for ever so long, and how that thing of yours has grown! That net-work chafed you, my dear, or it would never get like that."

Saying which, she made me lay by her side, clasping me tightly to her bosom, which heaved tumultuously. "Poor thing, how hard and swollen it is," she said, putting her hand on my affair. "Let me soothe it; there— there—there, it will be all right soon," but I could feel her heart beating furiously, whilst her beautiful face was aflame, and those deep blue eyes seemed to dart sparks of love as she regarded me. Imperceptibly I was drawn between her legs, and my tool throbbed against her belly. "There is only one away, Percy, to cure that stiff thing of yours; let me put it somewhere for you, my dear;" I was passive in her hands, and she presently placed the head of my Prick just inside her moist warm Cunt, for she had been spending in anticipation, the effect was electric as far she was concerned, her bottom gave one big upward heave, and I felt myself at last buried to the hilt inside my own Mother. "Mamma Mamma, where have you put it? It feels so warm and nice."

"Oh, my own boy, my Percy, I must have you; push it all into me, dear. I must teach you; you will find it delicious to be cuddled in that way; Ah, my love, my own boy, let me feel your soul flow into mine; let me make you feel what real love is like."
"Mamma, Mamma darling, how nice! What are we doing to each other?"

"Making love, Percy dear, don't you like it?" as she pressed me closer and tighter in her arms every moment, whilst her hot swimming Cunt sucked me in ravenously at each thrust I gave.

"Making love is nice; may I often do it to you, Mamma?"

"Yes, my lovely boy, only never let a soul know it; it is thought so improper, but now Percy, now push it all in—faster faster; I give you my very life. Oh—Oh—I'm coming; can't you feel my warm flow?"

"Yes—yes, what is going to happen, Mother—Mamma I shall burst.— Ah—there it is—Oh," as I had played my part to the end, and was fairly exhausted by the spend and the intensity of my emotions.

Her arms held me tightly to her bosom, as she panted after her excessive lubricity, keeping me still on the top of her, whilst the contractions of her vagina treated my Prick to the most exquisite compressions. I put one hand down to feel where I was, and ran my fingers all round the lips of her salacious Cunt, putting them up inside as far as they would reach. "Let your hand play with me, and move yourself on me at the same time; let me teach you how to please your Mother, who loves you so; do you know Percy, I have given you my very life, my honour,—fancy a boy like you putting horns on the head of his Father!"

"Mamma, dear, what do you mean, you talk so funny, how can I make horns for Papa?"

"By what you are doing my love, by perhaps making me a baby; you will understand some day."

"And would a baby be a brother, just like me?"

"Yes love, a brother or a sister—but Percy never a word to any one, as you love me; this is so naughty, so wicked to do."

"Naughty, wicked, how can it be so to play with my Mamma!"

"Fathers or Mothers must not have their children like this, nor even Brothers their Sisters; it is thought awful called 'Incest' in fact.
The Clergyman would say we were cursed—but that is all nonsense. We know better; it's their business to call everybody sinners."
My Prick was now going great guns once more, swelling and poking her to perfection.

"How long I have waited for this! Do you know what you are doing to me,
Percy."
"No, Mamma, what do you call it, and what is the name of the beautiful place you put me in?"

"It's 'Fucking', that is the word for it, and you are in my Cunt, dear."

"Then I'm Fucking my own Mother, and my affair is pushing into her Cunt; it is nice, Mamma."
"Yes, Heavenly, and call your affair your Prick; you have a grand Prick for your age, my boy. Fuck me, shove it up as far as it will go at every stroke you give. You can't hurt my Cunt; it will take your hardest poking, the more vigorous you are, the greater the pleasure; then when we come together, it is the greatest possible bliss. Love your Mother, I have given all to possess my boy."

"What a glorious Mamma, and how I love her; you make me feel a very part of yourself."

She heaved in response to every dig, faster, more furiously Fucking every moment, till we both spent at the same instant, and my Prick revelled in a very ocean of sperm, and we lay faint and spun out by our exertions. "Let me look, Mother dear, I want to see where I am," I presently said, throwing off the sheet which covered us, and then for the first time had a realistic view of her belly and swelling mount, covered with a luxuriant growth of reddish-golden hair; my fingers instantly sought to part the curls which encircled my Prick, and drawing out a little I could see the clinging vermilion lips of the maternal vagina, which held on to my shaft, as if loth to part with its prize. For a moment or two I continued the slow in and out motion to see how it acted, but that was all she would permit, assuring me further exertion just then would be too much for me.—"Percy, I must mind you don't injure your health, so you must rest a little, then perhaps tomorrow, my love."

She gave me a glass of liqueur, which made me all on fire to possess her again; but she would not listen to anything of the kind, ordering me to have a good ride on my pony before luncheon. It was a bracing ride, but my thoughts were too distracted to think of anything but my Mother, and I returned possessed by a Fucking Devil to surprise Patty sleeping on Mary's bed, having undertaken to make the beds in her absence, and knowing I was out, she was having a quiet nap. Looking at her for a moment, my Prick stood at the thoughts of the charms under her shirts, so gently lifting them, I saw she had no drawers on, only nice stockings and slippers, but just then she opened her eyes. "Oh, Master Percy, no, you shan't," trying to put her skirts down,—but I had the advantage, and keeping her down, said: "You looked at me, now I will see all you have Patty, and kiss it, too." She struggled, but did not cry out, and I succeeded in kissing her naked thighs, whilst her hands covered her Fanny, so throwing myself by her side, I tried all I could to inflame her desires, by kissing her lips, which she returned, and then getting bolder, pushed my tongue between her lips, and she soon began to get quite hot and flushed: then now I was not attempting to look, my hand had better success below, slowly overcoming all obstacles, till I got a finger in her slit, and began to rub the ticklish spot of love. She gave a long deep sigh, and sucked in my tongue, the tip of her own meeting mine in the most amorous manner; I took one of her hands and placed it on my trousers just over where my Prick was throbbing in expectation, she gave a start and I let it out, placing it in her hand, "Oh, Patty," I whispered, "won't you make me happy, you feel how it is, dear."

"Oh, Master Percy, I'm afraid, I never did such a thing; oh, let me go; pray, pray, do!" taking her hand away, and trying to get up; but I had got one leg between hers, so rolling over on top of her, tried to push my advantage.

"Never, never;" she almost screamed, "I'll shout out if you try to."

But having gone so far, and being quite furious with lust for a Fuck no matter who, if only nice; I pushed ruthlessly, holding her in my arms like a vice, whilst by sucking and tonguing her lips, I kept her from screaming. Nature assisted me a little. The girls own emotions made her spend and I knew it by the deep drawn respiration and the quivering of her frame, as the spasm came. My Prick had got its head just inside her crack, when the soothing emission came opportunely to assist his progress, and tight little virgin as she was, desperately writhing and struggling under me, my charger gradually won his way, till furiously plunging and drawing her to me with all my strength, the hymen was broken through, as she screamed and sobbed for me to spare her; but I pushed on, tearing and stretching her tender passage; although so young, my big Prick was quite too much for her; at length all was over. I came, I saw and I conquered, shooting my love balm into her wounded Cunt for a second time before I would let her get up; not till then did I feel sorry for the ruin I had effected, but her sobs were so genuine I did all I could to soothe her, and promised to be more loving and gentle another time. "Ah, you bad boy, I don't know if I shan't tell your Mamma." "I'll never forgive you," she said, when at last she stopped crying before leaving the room.

My tool was blood-stained, so I carefully sponged it and looked to see if there were any other evidences of Patty's rape on the bed, but fortunately her clothes had saved that.

I was rather late for luncheon. Mamma looked so lovely and fresh, her blue eyes beamed love on me at every glance, and she supplied me with the most nourishing delicacies besides two or three glasses of champagne. She asked me how I had enjoyed my riding.—"Oh, it was delightful, Mamma," I said thinking of her and Patty.

"Percy, will you read to me, dear, this afternoon as I want to get on with a bit of work for the bazaar. You know Mr. Pokemall will be angry with me if I don't do something for the vicarage stall."

"Couldn't you pacify him, Mamma?"

"Percy, don't be sarcastic, I hate the sight of him, only we must appear to be good."

She took me to her boudoir, which made me think of Mary's tale. "Oh, if the couch could tell me all it knew!" I thought.

Seated on a stool at her feet I read from Ouida's "Moths" for a little but she did not care for that, so asked me to look into Zola's "Nana" and read about her love for Satin. "But Mamma, Satin was a girl, what could she do to make Nana love her so?"

"They were Lesbians, my dear, girls who prefer sucking and kissing each other to being fucked by a man."

"Mamma, do you like your Cunt kissed? Let me do it for you."

She did not reply, but threw her skirts over my head, as I sat below her on the stool, putting me at once into darkness, and almost driving me wild as I sniffed the mixed aroma of her perfumed Cunt; my hand groped along her thighs, feeling how soft they were, encased in what I believed to be the same openwork tights I had tried on in the morning, but they fitted so closely, I could not get fairly at her. However, not to be baffled, I got my fingers inside and split them up, then my lips sought her mossy-covered mount, and my tongue found her hot, moist slit, all dripping with the creamy emission she had already discharged, working its way as she now opened her legs to facilitate my operations. How eagerly my mouth sucked her clitoris, which I kept between my lips, as she wriggled with pleasure, and I could feel her hands outside, pressing my head to keep me there—sucking—sucking, I rolled the fleshy morsel in my mouth and titillated it with my tongue; at the same time, at first one, and then two fingers found their way into her bottom-hole, the muscle of which held them tenaciously, as they frigged her rapidly. "Ah—Oh—Oh, you love of a boy!" I heard her cry. "Frig me, suck me. I'm spending. Oh—Ah!" And a flood of sperm gushed all over my lips and chin, as I swallowed all I could catch in my mouth. I never gave up working on that delicious clitoris, and even gave little bites now and then, as she reclined backward, sighing each time I slightly relaxed my efforts. "More, more, more, my love!" till at length, mad with desire, I jumped up and rammed my excited Prick into her reeking cunt, just in time to let her have the benefit of my emission.

My lips and mouth were all covered with sperm, but quite regardless of that she kissed and sucked my lips in the most lascivious manner, keeping my cock tightly imprisoned in her tight fitting sheath, which seemed able to take in and keep possession of any sized tool.

A very short time sufficed to start us on again, and another most delicious Fuck rewarded me for all my first loving attentions to her Cunt.

"What a fucker you are, Percy; only to think I never had you before to day.—My mouth, my tongue, my bosom, my cunt, even my arse, shall be all yours; now I spend—Fuck—shove your balls into your mother, she is all yours, Percy."

"And how I love to fuck you, Mamma. My prick is all for you heavenly Cunt; am I pleasing you, darling mother? Have I learned to fuck properly? May I dress up in your chemise and drawers again? Do I make a pretty girl?" And I went on, making my Prick revel in that swimming cunt, till the floodgates of love opened and a rush of my sperm assuaged her burning lust for the time. Still she wanted to take my cock in her mouth, but as it was limp, I tucked it away between my legs, laughingly pretending to be a girl, as I really knew I had done enough for that day at least.

Thus ended my first day's enjoyment of my Beautiful Mother. In another volume I purpose to write the Further Adventures of a Precocious Boy, and after that go on to the Secret of my Life up to present time.

FINIS

MORE FORBIDDEN FRUIT OR

MASTER PERCY'S PROGRESS

In and beyond

the Domestic Circle

MORE FORBIDDEN FRUIT

MY BEAUTIFUL MOTHER

My mother was too wise to allow Mary to sleep in the same room with me after having, as she thought, opened my eyes and allowed me to taste the forbidden fruit of love. That night I was glad to retire early and went to sleep fully believing my usual bed-fellow would lay herself by my side when she returned home with my aunt; but I slept soundly till the next morning and was greatly surprised to find myself alone when I awoke in the morning, and lay for some time wondering how it was—supposing of course they had stayed at my aunt's friends all night. About eight o'clock there was a tap at the door, and I called out "Come in!" and there was Patty all blushes and smiles to say it was nearly breakfast time.

"Here, Patty," I said, holding out my arms to her, "Come and forgive my rudeness to you yesterday. Kiss me; then I shall be sure you do."

"How can I help loving you, Master Percy, after what you did to me?" as she threw her arms round my neck and imprinted a long, burning kiss on my lips.

"You didn't have Mary here last night; your Mamma made her sleep with her last night, and they are not up yet, so I made a pretence to call you. I couldn't get you out of my thoughts all night, you wicked, bad boy. Now you have ruined me."

45

"My love, how could I help it? You looked so tempting as you lay asleep on the bed," I said, getting one hand up her clothes till it fairly grasped her mossy palpitating love grot.

She didn't struggle, but said softly: "Ah, no, you mustn't, you'll make me a baby, Percy; you are such a big, strong fellow."

"You don't love me, Patty, or you would want me again, but I mean to have it now, just this once, my darling, so don't make a fuss, I must have you now," pulling her down by my side as I threw off the sheet, which was all I had over me, and exposed to her view my Prick in a most glorious state of erection.

There was no resistance now, as I made her grasp the staff of life and champion of love in her hand. "What a big thing!" she whispered. "Only to think it has been in me, or I should be dreadfully frightened, you bad, bad boy," she whispered, gluing her lips to mine in a long, ardent kiss. It was too delicious to hurry matters, her hand was gently, and I believe instinctively, caressing my delighted Prick, which seemed ready to burst from excessive desire, as our tongues met in rapturous dartings in and out of each other's mouths. She heaved a deep sigh, and knowing the psychological moment had arrived with her, I rolled over between her legs, and her own fingers, directed by the intensity of her feelings, put the head of my affair well within the lips of her swimming Cunt, one or two easy shoves sending it home to her heart's desire, as she heaved up to meet the penetrating strokes.

"Ah, how lovely, to feel it all in me again! You don't know how I have longed for you once more. Percy darling, since you ruined me yesterday. Ah, that was awful, how you stretched and tore into my poor Pussy, and yet, you bad boy, I loved you for it, I wanted it so; why didn't you run after me when I run away from you in the corridor at first? But I guess it was Mamma you were after just then, dressed as you were in her things. The sight of you and that kiss did make me feel hot. Now tell me everything, or I will shove you off, and you shan't have any fun with me."

46

I had got her too tight, but to please her and add zest to my fucking, I told her what a love my mother was, and how we had enjoyed ourselves in her bed, adding, "No fear, I shall fuck every one in the house now, neither my mother or my aunt shall stop me now I have found out what a pleasure it is."

"You dear boy, Percy. I must have my share, even if you make me a baby: shove into me! Quicker! Faster! Fuck me hard! Ah! oh! it's coming again. Spunk into your Patty. Say you will love me a little."

My boiling hot sperm shot into her delighted cunt at that same moment, making her squirm with the excess of her emotion, but it never relaxed in stiffness and kept on poking away, and making her more and more excited till we both came again in a perfect flood of love juice, which was so profuse that my balls and thighs, as well as her notch and legs, were all drowned in the creamy, viscous fluid and we lay panting and exhausted. There was no time for further fucking just then, so I rushed off to the bath-room to refresh myself.

Aunt Gertie was my sole companion at the breakfast table, and she eyed me with a peculiar look as I hungrily put away a lot of devilled kidneys, as well as two raw eggs beat up and mixed in my coffee, to which she slyly added a little fine old Cognac, a speciality of my father as a pick-me-up after too much woman.

"Percy," she said archly, "Did you miss Mary last night? Mamma took care to keep her away from you now she thinks she has opened your eyes. I knew she would take advantage of our being away yesterday to take what she thinks was your maidenhead, but we know better, don't we, dear. Still you must give Auntie Gertie her due now and then, as I taught you first. Tell me how she seduced you, Percy."

"Oh, Gertie, you know I was mad for her and didn't wait for her to give me a chance. I went and caught her asleep, so I dressed up in her chemise and that blue open-work combination, slippers, stockings, and all: it did show everything off, and the size of my bursting prick made her eyes start, I can tell you. Yet I pretended to not know anything, and acted the innocent so well she thinks she taught me everything. Ah! it was lovely—luscious—I can tell you; so I didn't want Mary much last night, you may be sure. But talking of it makes me awfully stiff now; let me kiss your lovely cunt, and have a fuck on the chair. We can't go anywhere else; the servants won't come unless rung for."

My head was soon under shirts, and my tongue made that lascivious cunt of hers quiver and spend in profusion, as I sucked out every drop, then jumping up, as rampant as a goat, I pulled her across my lap as I sat on a chair; her hands taking hold of my terribly rigid instrument and holding it straight to the mark, as she slowly impaled herself on it; then, gluing her lips to mine, she almost sucked my breath away as she rode up and down on my champion. We were both too hot for it to last long, her spendings gushed in response to my emission at the critical moment, and we revelled in a sea of delight, her cunt nipping me so tightly that I kept on tossing her up and down on it, and a long drawn out engagement made us both so excited that when we spent again the erotic fury gave me such strength that I fairly lifted her in my arms as I stood up and danced her on my prick, without any support from the chair, till I reeled back spent and exhausted, dragging her to the floor by my side. How we laughed when we recovered a little, and resolved to have many more such fucks after breakfast when Mamma happened to lay late.

"Now I shall go and have a look at them in bed, and, if Mary is still with Mamma, will get in between them. Won't that be a lark, Gert?"

"What a boy my Percy is," she said, kissing me. "Take a drop of Papa's liqueur, and perhaps, after all I have done, you will be able to do as much as she can expect after what she did for you yesterday."

I had a nip of that wonderful liqueur, which must have been the same as Mary had mentioned when telling me of the scene between Capt. Devereux and his sisters, for it fired my blood, and if my aunt had not

48

vanished I should have been into her again, so powerful was the aphrodisiac effect.

My prick was as rampant as ever, so I dashed away to my room, stripped quite naked and throwing a dressing-gown around me, hurried to Mamma's bed-room. Entering very stealthily, I surprised her and Mary in the midst of a Tribadic scene each with her head buried between the other's thighs and busy sucking the love-juices as greedily as possible. The bottom nearest to me happened to belong to darling Mary, and the sudden fancy possessed me to put my eager prick into the lovely little brown hole which Mamma's finger was just then probing rapidly, to the girl's evident delight, judging by the way she swayed her buttocks about and pressed down her cunt reciprocating every touch of tongue, mouth, or busy fingers.

Dropping my dressing-gown. I was there in a moment. One hand pulled back my Mamma's fingers as the other presented the head of His Randiness to the wrinkled, brown bum hole of Miss Mary, which was fairly lubricated by the finger-frigging it had had, and got the head of my prick really lodged within the tight entrance before the girl was aware of what was happening.

Mamma realised the situation at once, as with a suppressed ejaculation of "Ah, rogue, push it all into her," she grasped poor Mary firmly round her waist, so she could not get away from me.

"Oh, Lord, what's that? How big it is. Ah, no, no, you shan't, Mr. Percy. Oh, Madame, pray don't let him do that to me," she almost screamed as she found out who it was and what I was at; but all her efforts to frustrate me were useless, as I held on tightly to her buttocks with both hands pulling her towards me, as my prick shoved his way gradually in, till I accomplished the ravishing of her second maidenhead. The state of extreme lubricity in which I had surprised her made my conquest easier than it might otherwise have been, and now I was in she soon began to get still more excited, and Mamma had no further occasion to hold her so tightly, and busied herself by kissing and caressing my balls as they

49

banged against the girl's bottom at every stroke. The liqueur I had taken had the effect of making me desperately stiff, although it did not hasten the climax, which to our mutual enjoyment was some time in coming off, and words fail me to describe the erotic ardour of this bottom-fuck; I ground my teeth like any one in a rage every time I plunged into that burning back passage of hers, and she seemed beside herself with emotion, squealing and sobbing from excessive pleasure, till at last my spunk squirted right up to her vitals, and I knew she also experienced the very acme of bliss, although it seemed to have been one long continued spend with her and my mother.

After enjoying the compressions of that delicious arsehole for a few minutes I withdrew with difficulty. My priapism continued so violent, and prick was so enormously distended that when at last it came out there was a flop like the drawing of a very tight cork.

Mamma seized my member and sucked it clean in her mouth, but finding there was not the least relaxation of stiffness wished also to have it in her bottom.

Mary could hardly yet believe that my now enormous tool had really been up her back entrance, so she wished to see the operation performed, and getting off Mamma, made her kneel up dog-fashion and taking her old friend in her hand, presented its head to my mother's bottom, as I mounted behind. It was not a virgin like Mary's and was well stretched by previous insertions of her husband's and other pricks; still my priapism continued so strong on me, and my affair was so enlarged, it was no very easy matter to shove past her tight sphincter muscle, which gripped the head of my prick and made further progress hard to achieve.

The idea of fucking my own mother's bottom increased my ardour, I felt actually stronger than ever, and should have liked to get in balls and all; her buttocks were pushed out to facilitate my efforts, and getting past that muscular obstruction, my cock glided in to the roots of my sprouting hair; what a luscious feeling that was; Mary was handling my

50

balls most lovingly, as she feared they might be lost inside, and I could feel her kissing my rump.

"Now it's all in. Fuck me well, Percy, my love! don't forget it's your own mother who gives all to her dear boy. Make it last as long as possible. Frig my cunt, Mary—put in two fingers. Now go on, but not too fast at first—gentle strokes bring the greatest pleasure, till at length we go crescendo. Oh, you do it so nicely, my love, my own boy! Isn't he a darling, Mary? He shall fuck you, my love, as often as he likes; only I must have my boy when I want him."

"Darling Mamma—my own mother. Do I do it nicely?" as my cock pushed slowly and gently in and out of that delicious bottom, which closed so tightly on my enraptured tool, feeling as hot as a fresh poultice; the grip on the sphincter muscle and the heat inside combining to produce the most voluptuous sensations.

I got beside myself with the erotic intensity of pleasure, and soon began a rather furious pushing; each drive increased my ardour, making her wriggle and squirm her buttocks about so that had I not got a firm grasp with my hands I should have lost my position. Mary's fingers frigged her rapidly as well, and she managed with her other hand to caress my testicles, and every now and then grasped the root of my prick, drawing back the skin of the foreskin, so that each plunge gave me the most intense delight, the head and shoulders of my prick being so well bared, I felt the contraction of her anus in the most exquisite degree.

My priapism was too violent for me to spend quickly, so this was a most delicious drawn out bottom-fuck, which seemed never ending to me, and I could feel dear Mary's fingers well up her cunt, as only the thin membrane was between them and my burning tool.

Sometimes she withdrew her fingers, all dripping with my mother's copious emissions, and tried to insert them by the side of my prick in the maternal arse-hole, but only succeeded in getting one up alongside of Mr. Pego; this was a lovely idea and tended even more to excite me.

"Spend, mother darling. Shove your bottom out to meet every poke I give you, I shall come soon now!" I almost shouted in my savage delight. "Fuck! Fuck! Fuck!—Ah, this is Fucking. It's come! Don't you feel it shoot up you, dearest mother? Oh, oh, I'm done now!" as I fell exhausted and rolled by her side on the bed.

She drew my face to hers between her two hands—laughing, sobbing, and crying from the excess of her feelings. "My boy, my own Percy, how you did fuck me, you dear," smothering me with a profusion of the most loving hot kisses, whilst Mary, also carried away by the scene in which she had participated, took possession of my still stiff machine and sucked it till she had extracted every drop that still oozed from it.

We had been nearly an hour over these two bouts of bottom-fucking, and now felt so done up we fell asleep in a confused heap of disorder, uncovered as we lay and our parts reeking with the overflow of so much spending.

It was long past mid-day when I opened my eyes again on the scene, Mary was gone, but darling Mamma was ardently examining my manly cock, feeling how stiff it was still, and gently frigging it with the softest possible up and down motion of her delicate hand, covering and uncovering the ruby-coloured head as her hand moved the skin.

"Let me feel your lovely cunt, my own mother's cunt," as I got my fingers between the pouting lips of her vermilion slit, working them gently so as gradually to again rouse all the lubricity of her nature. Within a couple of minutes a flood of sperm rewarded my efforts to please her, and she gasped in ecstasy: "What a boy you are! There is such a magnetism in your touch, I came directly. In fact, the idea of possessing you, my lovely boy, makes me spend continuously. I even kept coming in the short sleep I have just had, and when I awoke your precious prick was still standing hard in my hand; you don't come often, and I am rather afraid of injuring you, my pet! but I must have it once more; once more

52

feel this fleshy jewel probing up towards my very heart. Lie still on your back and take it as easy as you can: I will do all the work."

Saying which she rolled me over, then kneeling across me, took my inflamed prick, now as hard as ivory, and placing the head to her longing notch, slowly settled her body down upon it as it gradually slipped in, and seemed to fill and distend even her well-used cunt—used as it had been to take in the manly affairs of husband, brother, or others.

"You dear boy, how your grand, young prick fills your mother. To think my boy is such a splendid fellow! What a fucker you will be!" she said laying herself over me and kissing my lips rapturously, but never for a moment allowing her glorious cunt to lose hold of my cock. Sitting up again, she slowly raised her buttocks up and down, so as to let me feel each insertion, nipping me so tightly that the folds of her vagina turned back the foreskin each time she came down on me. This fired me so I could not keep still, but grasping her round the hips, I bucked up to meet each downward motion, sending my delighted tool chock up to the entrance of her womb. Now and again she settled down on me in the closest possible conjunction and treated my prick to the most enjoyable contractions on the very head of my bursting engine, till at length quite a sudden paroxysm made me eject right into her womb as she imparted to me a most singular quivering sensation, the sure indication to both of us of a real impregnation.

"You've done it again, Percy. I shall have twins, and if they are girls you shall fuck them as soon as they are old enough," she said with a laugh. "But really, my darling, I should like my own boy to make me a baby— you would be both father and brother to it. Now we must get up for luncheon or Aunt Gert will be after us. She always knew I would have you, and you may have her some day."

"You lovely mother," I said, clinging to her for another kiss. "I shall fuck you all in this house. I know I shall, now I think of nothing else. There's you, auntie, Mary, and Patty. I must have her too. May I Mamma?"

"What a boy it is: but you must always love Mamma best, Percy, won't you?"

"Yes, darling mother; but you have taught my prick to fuck, and—and I want so to shove it into every nice woman or girl I see. I know I shan't be able to help myself."

"To-night you are to sleep in that room next to mine, and I won't let you do any more for a day or two: you must not be exhausted by too much of it, or you will soon be ruined in your health. So I must now keep you away from Mary, as your eyes are opened to the forbidden fruit."

However inclined I might be for the incestuous embraces of my lovely mother, the door being locked on the other side, it could only be when she thought proper to admit me, as she intended to have due regard for my health, and not allow a boy of my age to run into excesses, which might ruin my constitution.

She could also now (as she thought) take care that neither of the others should rob her of very much of my puerile vigour, which was so precocious considering my age. For a day or two her precautions were quite needless, as when my violent priapism had subsided it left my energies in a very relaxed state, and I would seriously advise any of my readers who may think of resorting to Aphrodisiacal stimulants, to have nothing to do with them, but rather to trust to the impulses of their nature; when they really need a good fuck the cock-stand will be evident enough; forcing nature only tends to after enervation, and should only be resorted to on some special occasion when one really wishes to prove himself a champion in the arena of Love. Then it may be excusable.

But to return to my story: I did not at all relish the idea of Mamma's supervision, it was repugnant to my idea of personal liberty, and had the contrary effect, in making me restive under such restraint, and firmly resolved to do as I liked every chance I could get. One morning I had a most pleasant dream. "I was in a beautiful garden, laying on the soft turf under some rose bushes, when just as I was hand-frigging myself two

54

delicious looking little girls stood before me, holding up their frocks, and showing me their rosebuds of hairless slits, as they also rubbed and frigged their little cunts, smiling and telling me they could. They were exquisitely dressed in the Watteau style, looking almost like Dresden figures, being so chic and delicate; then, seating themselves one on each side me on the grass, they proceeded to handle and play with my great big prick, allowing me at the same time to frig their two little cunts for them, till the juice spurted from my affair right up into their faces, and I could feel their sticky young spendings all over my busy fingers." I awoke and found I had quite deluged the sheet with a flood of sperm. This dream made me reflect and think where such little dears could be found. I was quite innocent as regards knowing what an awful offence it would be to poke or take liberties with such little girls, so resolved to take a walk in search of adventures.

Our residence stood in large grounds of its own, surrounded by a delightful country stretching away in a long vista to the South Downs. Papa owned several farms in the neighbourhood, so we were generally respected and looked up to by the working class and their families, as Mamma disbursed a good deal in helping any who might be in trouble.

I remembered one labourer's family, the husband a carter who never got home till late in the evening, as his work was rather at a distance; his wife, about thirty or a little more, was a fine, handsome, young woman with a ruddy, tanned face, but oh! such brown eyes as she looked at you from under her dark eyelashes. She was a fine woman of her class, and I had once heard Mamma say Peter, her husband, had to marry Phoebe (that was her name) very young as he had got her into trouble; she had three very pretty little girls—ten, eleven, and twelve years old—regular beauties, with the same dark brown eyes and arch looks as their mother, and they were well grown for their ages. This was my mark. I had often been with Mamma on a visit to their cottage when they had any little illness, and carried a basket of nice things for them. I didn't know their family name, but Phoebe always kissed me and so did the girls when they were well. "Master Percy, Master Percy," they would call out as soon as ever I got in sight, because I generally had some sweets in my pocket for them. Now I had not been to the cottage for quite two years, and wondered if Phoebe would kiss me now. I would her if I got the chance. It was only about a mile to walk from our house down an unfrequented lane leading to nowhere but an old farm-house further on.

Mrs. Twiggs, our housekeeper, lent me a small basket, so I went into the pantry and helped myself to a good sized cake, some eggs, and a bottle of port wine, as I said I had heard that Phoebe was rather delicate.

I timed myself to get to the cottage soon after their mid-day meal, so as to have a long afternoon in case I found any sport.

Phoebe was all smiles as she answered my rap at the cottage door. "Oh, Master Percy, how you have grown, and how's your Mamma—I hope she isn't ill?"

"No thanks, Phoebe, I heard you were not quite well, so made up my mind to walk over with some new-laid eggs and a bottle of wine for you and a cake for the girls; where are they?"

"How kind of you, Master Percy, who could have told you that? I'm all right, and the girls have gone to see their grand-mother at Becton and won't get home much before dark, so I'm alone; no-one ever comes so see me. Thank you so much. Won't you come in and sit down for a rest?"

"That I will, Phoebe, and I feel done up carrying that basket. You might draw the cork and give me a glass of port, and a drop will do you good."

The cork was soon drawn, and she drank to my health with her "Best respects to you, Master Percy. How you have grown, I shan't like to kiss you now."

"Why not, Phoebe, what harm can it be? I have often sat on your lap and kissed you when my mother was here, and I mean to again."

"Oh, no, it isn't proper only with little boys. They're harmless you know; now you're so big you must only kiss your young lady sweetheart, or Mamma, or your dear aunt, Miss Gertie."

"But you must give me one, or I shall feel quite a stranger. What harm can it be?"

"Well I don't know any harm, and you're a dear, kind boy to think of us, as you have, but I mustn't do it again before any one," as putting her glass down she stood up and kissed my cheek, and would have sat down again; but my arm was round her waist in a moment, drawing her close to me, my lips kissed hers, then her cheeks and lips again.

"You only gave me half a kiss, Phoebe, I must have a proper one," pushing her back on her chair, and seating myself on her lap. "This is how I want it, just as you used to do. Now kiss me nicely."

Her rich-colored face crimsoned, and I felt her splendid bosom heave with emotion as I fairly glued my lips to hers, and tried to push my tongue between her lips, and one hand tried to get inside her neck-kerchief.

"You mustn't, you wicked boy. What a flutter you have put me into: now get away do, Master Percy. You ought not to kiss me like that."

But she only struggled faintly; my hand slipped inside her bosom and felt those still lovely firm orbs, as her heart palpitated and her lips gradually relaxed till my tongue fairly met hers tip to tip.

"Ah, you rogue! how bad you make me feel," returning my caresses, and rubbing one hand up and drown my back, as if she only wished she dared put it in front.

"Percy, Percy, Master Percy, for shame, don't be so rude," as I suddenly placed her hand on my big prick which I had let out of my trousers. "What a size for a boy of fourteen, and I believe you know a lot."

"Yes, Phoebe, I know what 'cunt' and 'fuck' mean; shall we have a game? We're all alone, and it is so nice—you have made me feel wild." I was now raising her skirts and soon had my hands up a splendid pair of thighs, fit for Venus herself, and quite innocent of drawers, as a delightful aroma of cunt made me feel still more randy. Separating her legs, as she lay back in the chair, I could see what a splendid white skin she had, and the lips of her cunt just peeping out from a profusion of almost black brown hair. Not a word passed between us as I tried to get into her, but I could hear the heavy breathing and the almost audible palpitation of her heart. I was a little awkward, but her hand helped me to go straight: the head of my eager prick got in, and, she pushing herself forward, I progressed upwards within the folds of her vagina and found myself at full length in one of the hottest cunts I had yet felt. "Wait a moment, don't hurry, dear; let me enjoy it—this is a treat, Master Percy. I couldn't help myself, but it is so awfully wicked you know."

She kept me like that for quite five minutes, the inner folds of that amorous cunt of hers pressing and nipping the head of my prick, her arms were tightly clasped round my back, so I could scarcely move, whilst her lips seemed as if they would eat mine, and her tongue was regularly fucking my mouth.

"Let me fuck you, Phoebe, you're making me come. I can't stop it, dear. Ah, oh! There it is shooting up you. Can't you feel it?"
"Yes, yes, I'm spending too, Percy, you love; what a grand prick to hold in my cunt—Peter's isn't near so big—you fill me up so beautifully, besides he only fucks me on Sundays; he is too tired to do it during the week. Will you come and see Phoebe as often as you can? Now fuck me well, you dear boy."

Without losing my stiffness, I went on drawing right out to the head of my instrument and pushing it slowly in again, which soon drove her quite wild.

"Faster quicker, fuck hard, darling!" she almost screamed, and as I did so with all my force, she lay back and gave quite a neighing squeal in the excess of her lubricity. I came again at the same moment. So finished my first fuck with the splendid country woman, who was indeed a rough jewel in her way. She would not permit any more just then, so I took leave of her after we had kissed each other's parts, and she made me promise not to be long before I called again.

All the way home my prick was very troublesome to me, I had not had enough; it repeatedly stood stiff so that I could hardly walk, and I think it must have been that, like many quiet women who seldom think their cunts require a bath, she had treated me to rather too much essence of woman.

Mamma made me read to her and Auntie after dinner till it was time to retire. My morning's adventure, as I thought over it and all the possibilities it promised for future pleasure (not only with Phoebe, but also her three girls) now roused me to a state of quite furious lust.

"Mamma, Mamma!" I shouted as I jumped out of bed and rattled at the door between our rooms. "Open, oh open, mother, I'm so ill!"

This ruse answered at once, and I found Mary was with her, as, opening the door, anxiously enquired what was the matter.

"Look, look, I shall die! It's so stiff," lifting my night shirt to let her see my glorious state of erection, as I rushed in and jumped on her bed, where I found darling Mary under the coverlet. Being mad for a fuck I tried to uncover her, but she rolled herself in the bed-clothes laughing at my baffled efforts to get at her.

"Help me, Mary, to hold him tight. I'll make his bottom tingle for cheating me like that," grasping me by her left arm round my waist and keeping me face downwards on the bed. "You're ill are you, Percy? Well I'm the doctor; a few good spanking slaps will do you good. Hold him tight, Mary, he's so strong and so wicked. There, there, how do you like that—and that—and that? Kick away my boy!" as I plunged and yelled under the smarting smacks.

"The poor boy; pray don't be too hard on him," said Mary, holding me tightly with both arms around my neck, and kissing me amorously at the same time.

"Well, well, you take his part, do you, you wanton girl? you are as bad as he is. No doubt this has been planned between you; have him then and see what you will get by it."

Mary disentangled herself from the coverlet, etcetera, and opening her delicious thighs, my randy weapon instantly found its way into her spending cunt, which was so well lubricated that the entrance was effected almost instantly, and she heaved up in delight as she felt the full insertion of the object she so desired. My mother was equal to the occasion, having perhaps even rehearsed it with her beforehand; taking two long long leather straps, she passed one underneath dear Mary's buttocks and buckled it tightly over my plump bottom, so that we could not enjoy the proper fucking motion, and in answer to our expostulations that it was too tight, quickly passed the second strap over my left shoulder bringing it back under her left and my right armpit.

Thus strapped together we could scarcely move, excepting our hands and feet.

"Mamma, Mamma, this isn't fair, how can we do it like that? I shall never come unless I can push it in and out properly; do, do, loosen the straps a little."

"Or, no, Percy, that is not my game; you'll spend soon enough, my boy."

She had now got a broad strap, something like the one to the window of a first-class railway carriage, made of tough, hard webbing, with a knotted, tasselled end.

"Look here," she said, "all you have got to do, is to roll over, so I can touch up first one and then the other; the uppermost bottom gets the worst of it, so it's a fine game both for me and you." Then a dull thud made me feel that strap. Thud! Thud! Thud! in succession, each blow a little harder. It not only made me smart and twist, but the knotted ends hurt amazingly.

Wriggling both hands feet, I tried to turn Mary over me, but she was strong and lithe as a cat. Both bums now caught it hot, the stinging thuds helped us to roll over one another, so that neither escaped the incessant attack of dear Mamma. After a few minutes the painful novelty wore off, and I awakened to the awfully nice sensations I was experiencing, for although debarred from proper fucking motions of the in and out thrust as usual, the way we twisted and the little, short perks each impact of the tawse gave to our buttocks made us more excited each moment; added to which, Mary's nutcrackers acted their part on the head of my member most deliciously. Needless to say the spending with both of us was continuous, and the emitted sperm fairly gushed from us at each jerk.

"Oh, Mary you darling, you love! Keep on. Mamma dear, you are giving us a lesson in pleasure. This beats all I have felt yet!" whilst Mary hugged me closer every moment, kissing my lips and cooing out her words of loving endearment.

I suppose it was quite a quarter of an hour before Mamma let us loose, and we lay pumped out in each other's arms.

"Now it is my turn, when you feel sufficiently recovered. Mary, never mind if his affair is not quite stiff. Use the tawse well and it will soon do its duty to me."

My late partner quickly got up, and with her dark eyes flashing excitement, rapidly adjusted the straps, and with her hand tucked my rather limp tool into the maternal notch, which felt as if boiling over with her hot emissions of semen.

Lips to lips, Ma and I sucked and tongued as the tawse descended rapidly on our twisting buttocks. Mary evidently meant to pay out her mistress as hard as she could now she was at her mercy, making her fairly gasp as the stinging thuds whacked on that glorious bottom, making it writhe and flinch at each blow, causing the maternal cunt to quiver and grip my stiffening member more and more tightly each instant.

The rigidity of my raging prick was almost painful; my previously exhausted forces requiring a long time to quite come to the spending point; but each flood of joy gushing from my mother added to my lustful sensations, till in about twenty minutes the flood-gates burst again in such a torrent that previous efforts seemed as nothing to it.

"Enough for this time, I think," gasped Mamma, as she pressed me in her arms, and tried all she knew, with the inner folds of her vagina, to squeeze out the very last drop of my young love-juice.

All three of us adjourned to the bathroom, and the rest of that day found us doing our best to recuperate exhausted nature.

Longing for another spree at Phoebe's cottage, I knew I must keep myself from excesses, so tried my best to remain quiet, going fishing or riding to pass the time: but at night I lay thinking of Phoebe and her three little girls. The idea so took my fancy I was mad to get at them.

At last the suspense was ended, and I found myself one day at the cottage door, with a basket of nice things requisitioned from the housekeeper, which she had packed up for me.

Phoebe, as soon as she saw who it was, throwing her arms round my neck, "Oh, you dear Percy, to think I have you again! but it's so unlucky, dear, you can't touch me to-day," she said, kissing me as ardently as ever. "Oh, isn't that a shame? To think I should be so, just when you come to see me."

This was a poser for me, as in my youthful ignorance I had never come across such an obstruction to pleasure before.

"Why, Phoebe, what do you mean? Look at my affair, how stiff it is as soon as you kissed me," pulling out Mr. Pego to broad daylight.

"For shame, Master Percy! the girls might see you, they are close by in the garden," and then taking me into her sitting-room, she blushingly explained in me the custom of women, as the Bible calls it.

"We can't do anything to-day, dearie, the three girls are about; it is holiday time and I never expected you."

"Oh, my Lord! what shall I do if I can't fuck some one? How I should like a game with your girls, and to feel their little cunts, even if I could not fuck them: look, Phoebe I've got six sovereigns in my pocket, you shall have it all, if you let me have a spree with them."

How her eyes glistened at the sight of so much gold, probably more than she had ever seen in her life before.

"Why, Percy, you are worse than an old man. Mr. Jones, our parson, is a bad'un, but you beat him. Three at once, oh my! He only fingers Patty now and then, but says the others are too young. Patty doesn't half like it, you know, but then it's a good thing for me, as when I go and row the parson about it he always squares me with half a sou, so I just smacks Patty's arse well and threaten to murder her if she says a word to any one. It won't do to kill the goose that lays golden eggs, but we must be careful. They are sure to be in mischief, so I will just run out and catch them at it. Then won't I let you see their pretty little arses well slapped; and it will make your cock stand—like a fine poker as it is. I generally have a family slapping after dinner on Sundays, it makes Peter so randy to see their little cunts and rosy red arses! Then I do get a rare rogering I can tell you, but not so good as yours, dear."

63

She soon fetched them in from the garden, all flushed and crying, having dropped on them just as the two younger ones were fighting Patty, and had boxed their ears all round. "Now, you little scratch cats, just wipe you faces and see how I will tingle your naughty bums before Mr. Percy, that will just make you nicely ashamed of yourselves."

Little Sue—the youngest, about ten—hid her face in her hands, she was so shamefaced to see me; but Phoebe brusquely, as if in great temper, first wiped their hands and faces with a wet towel, then noticing the disorder of their little frocks, proceeded to divest them of everything, till they stood reduced to their smocks, shoes, and stockings.

"Did you ever see such dirty, bad behaved girls, such naughty little things, Master Percy? Oh, I don't know how to keep my hands off them, no slapping would half punish them enough," she said, dragging Sue across her lap. "Look at the dirt all up to her knees and thighs, she must have been crawling on the ground. Oh, you dirty young slut!" Smack, smack, smack, on her plump little thighs: the child screaming: "Oh mother! Mother don't Oh, don't, I will be better! Oh! I will!" as Phoebe still more exposed the quivering bum to my gaze, slapping Sue's bottom without mercy. It was indeed a sight to excite any one, as I could see everything, the crack of her bottom, and just inside that the little hairless slit opening a wee bit every time she writhed and twisted under that painful slapping.

Almost throwing the child from her, Phoebe, seeming in a terrible temper, proceeded to serve Minnie, the next one, in the same manner, whilst I took Sue on my knee to soothe her and kiss the tears from her eyes, passing my hands under her smock to feel the beautifully firm flesh all over her palpitating and still quivering body. But although fondling the little chit, and taking every possible liberty fingers could indulge in, my eyes followed every slap that the mother almost savagely laid on to Minnie's pretty bottom. Lovely sight to watch the tearful, screaming girl, with her nut-brown face, which made a lovely contrast to the whiteness of her skin below and the rosy red look of the well-spanked bum. "There, there, there," she said, out of breath, as the last three hard slaps were laid on to her screaming victim. "Now go to Mr. Percy to comfort your smarting arse, if he can."

"Poor little darling, Minnie, come to me, dear, and let Percy kiss your tears away. Never mind if I have seen your naughty bum, you won't fight Patty any more, will you?"

Her crimsoned, dark face, gave me a peculiar pleasure as I looked at it, so drawing her close to my lips, I kissed her cheeks and sucked her mouth till the little thing quivered with emotions she had never felt before, which increased more and more as I placed one of her little hands inside my trousers, making her feel my awfully stiff member.

"Oh, what is that, Mr. Percy?" she lisped. "Will it hurt me?"

"No, my pet; pass your hand over it, backwards and forwards; it is so nice for me. Don't be afraid. Don't you like me to tickle you as well?"

"Yes, yes," she said in a whisper, a still deeper blush coming over the brown face: "I do, it makes me feel hot all over and forget the smart of my bottom," returning kiss for kiss with girl-like ardour, "and it makes me love you so, Oh! I do love you, Percy, dear."

"What's that you have got, Min?" said Sue. "See the rosy red head as the skin rubs back. Let me feel it, do."

"Yes, do, Sue. Kiss it and play with it. Your soft, little hands will just do the trick for me."

Almost directly the spend came in a flood of spouting jets, right over Sue's face and both their hands, whilst the sight of it seemed to drive their mother wild, as struggling with the big Patty, to get at the girl's backside, she tore her smock off her, and, getting hold of a thin cane, began to cut poor girl's bottom without mercy, each cut raising a fiery-looking mark, which soon puffed up into a regular weal. Her victim screamed fearfully, but it did not effect her mother, who seemed carried away by her lustful fury, and the cottage being quite isolated, no one was at all likely to hear anything. At length she laid Patty on a bed which was in a recess screened by curtains, which she drew aside, and as the poor girl lay on her face, sobbing as if her heart would break, Phoebe called me to inspect the effects of her handiwork.

The bottom still quivered, and the weals were beginning to turn a darker red colour, and would probably be blue when a day old.

"Look! Look! Mr. Percy," said she, "haven't I just punished well. I guess Mr. Jones would about like that sight and to put his fingers in the crack as she lays there."

"Ah!" I replied, "poor thing. Let me kiss it for her. My tongue is far better than any parson's finger, and will soon make her forget all the pain."

"Kneel up, quick Patty, across the bed, with your knees on the edge, so Mr. Percy can kiss where I have hurt you. Now be sharp about it, or you will get the cane again."

She was too frightened not to do so at once. Besides she knew I was kind to the others, and her delicate, wealed bum was a thing to pity, but full of delight for me. My tool was again standing furiously, and I had thrown off both jacket and vest. There was just the slightest suspicion of down growing on the unfledged cunny, which was quivering and glistening on the pretty rose-like, pinky opening, as if the little bitch had actually had a slight emission. Mad with lust, I glued my lips first to that delicious-looking little pussy and sucked for all I was worth, whilst Phoebe, kneeling down, had my prick in her warm mouth, which I fucked in and out of as her tongue did its duty by rolling round its head. Patty squirmed in ecstasy. Phoebe sucked, and I spent a flood of love juice down her throat, whilst the two little ones, not to be out of the game, had pulled down my trousers and lifted my shirt behind, so as to pat and kiss my bottom, one on each side, making indeed a voluptuous experience for me.

"When a little recovered from the excitement of the foregoing tableaux, Phoebe made each of the girls take the head of my member in their mouths and suck it a little, whilst their hands fondled the bag of precious stones below, and when I was sufficiently worked up for another bout, she sat on the edge of the bed, standing Patty quite naked on a footstool between her knees, with her buttocks presented to me, said:

"Now, sir, I know you won't be satisfied till you have her, so put your randy affair in behind, along the parting of her bottom, and fuck as if you were really in her little cunt. Nip your thighs well together, Patty; it won't hurt you, and be as nice as you can about it, then you will feel and enjoy the pleasure."

Following her directions, I pushed along the crack straight under her bum, and felt Phoebe's hand grasp the head of my member each time it was pushed home; Patty, by her mother's directions, working her bottom to meet each thrust, and add to the illusion. My emission all went into the palm of Phoebe's hand, she rubbing it all up under the girl's little cunt. This was the end of that day's fun, and Phoebe assured me we might go a little further another time, and that there was no fear of the girls telling tales, as they were too much afraid of what their little arses would suffer if they did.

Nothing of moment happened for a short time after this, till going one day unexpectedly to stables, I heard Patty's voice talking to her brother, who was our groom. The window was open and one corner being shaded by the foliage of a Virginia creeper, I could both have a good peep and hear everything.

"Well, you do look after your brother, Pat: only I wish you had brought something stronger than the housekeeper's mild ale," he was saying.

"She says beer, this hot weather, is bad for everybody, especially young people, it makes their blood hot, so they get into mischief. What does she mean, George?"

"Well, girls are something like Master Percy's little mare there: do you see how she is twitching her tail—it isn't the flies, there's none in the stable—and I expect you feel something like that, don't you, Pat, now and then?"

She blushed up to her eyes, but said, innocently enough: "Tell me what you mean, George, why does she frisk her tail so?"

"She wants the horse, and I expect you do, too, this warm weather."

"Oh, you wretch, to talk like that as if girls ever think such things. It's all because you young fellows are always trying to ruin us girls." "Yes Pat, and if you were not my sister you would never get out of this stable all right, I'd horse you to your heart's delight."

"Don't be so rude, George, you make me feel quite all-overish like. There, don't kiss and squeeze me so: for shame, to do that to your own sister!" as he clasped her round the body, pressing her to his bosom, and smothered her face with kisses, as his hands were feeling the girl's plump, firm buttocks.

She did not struggle much, but it made her heave one of those deep-drawn sighs, which too plainly told it was all over with her.

"Oh, George, don't, if you were some other nice young man as good-looking as yourself I would not answer for what might happen just now, you made me have such a funny feeling."

"Between your legs, wasn't it, Pat? you're just like Master Percy's little mare, see how excited she gets when I touch her!" Keeping his arm round her waist, he drew the trembling girl close up to the hind quarters of the mare, then releasing his arm, he stroked the beautiful creature's rump with his hand, till the mare's tail whisked more than ever. Presently he put his fingers right into the mare's cunt, and worked them by thrusting in and frigging the twitching lips of that hyper-sensitive organ to the evident delight of the beast, to judge from the way she stood to allow it: at first his fingers simply glistened with the moisture of the aperture, which could be seen contracting and twitching spasmodically as his fingers increased the animal's excitement, till a gush of horsey lubricity sent quite a flood of thick creamy looking stuff all over his hands, the mare giving quite a low whinney from excess of pleasure.

"Poor thing, she wanted it. Don't you think so, Pat?" he said, wiping his hands on a handkerchief.

This scene appeared to drive all sense of modesty out of Patty's mind, for with a laugh on her flushed face she replied: "Not more than you do, George, my boy, to look at something swelling inside your breeches. I believe you have often horsed that mare yourself."

"Maybe I have, she makes me so randy swishing her tail about and stinging my face as I rub her down."

"How I should have liked to see that, and shall just find a peep-hole to watch how you go on. It will be rare fun if you don't know."

"How about yourself, Pat? If you could peep at that, you may as well look at this now; what do you think of your brother's cock, my dear?" as he let out to full view a fine standing tool of nearly eight inches long and thick in proportion, with the foreskin well turned back behind the fiery, ruby-coloured head.

It was plain to see there was incest in the air, she was all of a tremble, yet did not withdraw her hand when he made her touch his rampant tool, which seemed to strangely fascinate her.

"Although we are brother and sister, why shouldn't I have you as well as any other fellow! How can I help loving you the same as any one else? Men and women are the only animals who think it wrong; they were never told not to marry their mother or their sister; that little mare there would only be too pleased if she could just have father or brother to

69

satisfy her warm feelings. There's no harm in it, Pat; only parsons make out everything is so wicked, even fucking, the greatest pleasure God ever gave us. Never mind them. Come on my girl, I must have it, I'm just wild for a put in!" at the same time gradually pushing her towards a long, broad, padded stool which stood in one corner, and was his usual seat when polishing the bits or harness, &c.

"What a shame? Do spare me, George, you know I can't help myself, you are so strong," as she sank on the stool and he pushed her backwards full length on it, his hands rapidly raising her skirts till I could see the thighs I knew so well, exposed nearly up to her nest, which was still hidden by the rucked-up drawers. Somehow she still kept her hand clasped on his member, and as he ruthlessly stretched her legs apart, getting between them, pushing aside the chemise which hid the object of his lust, she ingenuously managed to direct his dart to the spot, murmuring: "Pray don't be rough, don't hurt me, George love, and you shall have your will of me."

He was certainly pushing for all he was worth, but clever girl as she was didn't want him to think he was not the first to take advantage of her virginity so her hand still retaining its grasp of his instrument, she squirmed and sighed: "Oh, oh, oh, its breaking! Stop you'll kill me, George!" then artfully letting him go, "Ar-r-r-re! Oh, you've forced it!" as he drove in till his hair rubbed against hers. She heaved her buttocks in ecstasy to meet his thrilling pushes, and in the midst of their excitement I slipped through the door and was close behind them, delightedly watching George's prick as it plunged in and out of Miss Patty's foaming little cunt just as they both seemed to spend together.

Guess their surprise and fright as I gave George a rousing slap on his arse. "You didn't know I was watching your game, my dears; what fun you were having, but where do I come in?"

George was out and too confused to put away his tool, which was now shrinking to its normal state, slightly hanging in a sort of semi-stiffness all dripping with spend whilst Patty still lay with her legs wide apart, showing her charms, with the roselike lips of her cunny all red and quivering from the recent excitement, whilst two or three thick drops of pearly spend were slowly dripping down towards the parting of her beautiful thighs.

"I've an idea how I can join in with you, she's not had half enough yet. George take her place on the stool and lay on your back, I want to see Patty ride on that fine prick of yours, and will tickle your balls and her cunt as I watch the game from behind. Now, my girl, mount upon him and open your legs well, the very idea has made him ready again."

"Oh, Mr. Percy, to think you should catch us doing such a wicked thing; we will do just what you order if you never tell. It was all George's fault. He would have me, indeed it was," she sobbed, two or three great big tears rolling down her flushed and shamed face.

"Don't tell fibs, Miss Patty, I saw it all from the beginning, and shall now punish you for forwardness and pert little saying, which only made him worse than he would have been. You know what he said was quite true, you are as bad as the animal there, which knows no better, whilst you could have run away and saved yourself if you had wished."

Whilst saying this to her, my hand had been holding George's throbbing tool as it stiffened up more and more every instant, then placing its head well within her grotto, lubricated as it was by her previous fucking bout, she settled herself down on John Thomas till he was all taken in, and with a deep-drawn sigh of pleasure, she threw herself forward to kiss him with all her ardour, thus exposing to my view a splendid sight of her bottom, pussy holding prick up as tightly as she could nip it, and all else.

"Gee-up—gee-up, little mare, laying still will never do, I'll make your arse ride him properly," as snatching up a band off a truss of straw which lay handy, I rope'sended her buttocks to perfection. She screamed, but George was enjoying it and clasped his arms tightly round her waist. The straw was so knotted and scratchy, it was no child's play for our victim. "Oh, oh, oh, for God's sake leave off, Mr. Percy," she whimpered, but it only made me go on worse, making me feel so awfully randy, my member was like a bar of iron inside my trousers.

They were both spending again, but I kept them on the go, the hard, knotted rope of straw paid into both of them without mercy till I thought I had done enough.

"That's for committing incest with your brother, you randy little mare. How did you like it? That straw rope was just the thing; now I will look at the damage. Oh! I have rather scratched the skin a bit, and there's lovely little drops of blood here and there, and so red all over; but my eye! how your cunt grips his prick, which is as hard as ever. Go on, Patty, fuck it out of him, there's nothing like riding St. George to pump up the spunk," I said, as my fingers pushed up inside her vagina alongside his tool, then as she winced a little, I rubbed some of the mixed spendings into the orifice of her wrinkled, tight-looking arse-hole, which, to judge by the way it spurred her on, increased the pleasure very perceptibly. My fingers, first one and then two, working into the nether aperture, enabled me to readily feel George's prick inside her cunt. This so inflamed my own passions, that unable to longer restrain myself, I brought the tip of my own member to the spot, and substituting it for the fingers, as my other hand lubricated the head with saliva, it went in about an inch, then clasping her firmly by the buttocks, I rammed in with all my strength. This sudden and unexpected attack, made her struggle to get away. "Oh, George, George, do let go, he's shoving his cock up my arse. I can't stand that! I must———."

"Hold tight George, never mind her, I've got her fine, it's awfully nice, and if you always have her this way, no harm can be done."

Just at that moment I shot a flood of spend right up her vitals, but my priapism was so intense the stiffness never relaxed, and both of us, George and self, revelled in all the lubricity of our young natures, whilst Patty went nearly mad, as she squirmed, squealed, and bit him in the excess of her emotions, being carried quite out of herself. This went on till we all three ejaculated and mixed the very essence of our natures, which left us to lay in an exhausted heap, one top of the other on the stool.

We all had a wash in a stable bucket of fresh water, and it amused me to see George use the big stable sponge to lave and cool Patty's excited parts. She was in a nervously lost kind of state, sobbing and whimpering: "Oh! oh! oh! You have quite done for me—my poor, poor bottom is so hot and so stretched—I shall never be right again. Oh! oh! oh! Kiss me, Mr. Percy. Kiss me, George. It was awfully grand—if I'm none the worse for it," as she felt herself getting better.

At length we thought she was well enough, so let her leave, taking a final embrace as she felt and squeezed our tools, saying: "You are two devils to serve a poor girl like that, I will never come near the stable again."

"Yes you will, Patty, next Sunday soon after breakfast, whilst most of them are gone to Church, and if I don't find you both here you will be served out for it."

This last experience of two males with a female quite tickled my fancy, so much so, that I resolved to ask Aunt Gert if she had ever had such a spree, and happening upon her in the garden a few hours later, I asked her to sit down and talk to me.

"Why of course I will, Perce, as you are such a nice boy, and take so little notice of your Auntie lately; Mamma and Mary seem to have the monopoly of your darling cockie, but you do thrive on it, my dear. Let me kiss you for once now I have the chance," throwing her arms round my neck and thrusting her tongue into my mouth as our lips met. We were near a handy bowery alcove at the end of a walk, in the most retired part of the garden, so that we could easily hear anyone approaching, and it was so closed in all round by a thick thorn fence, with a wall behind, that no one could creep close enough to spy upon persons there.

Drawing me upon her lap, one hand found its way inside my pants and brought forth M. Pego, who stood at attention the moment his services seemed likely to be required.

"Look, Perce, how imprudent he is to stand like that in my face, what a darling prick! Oh, you dear boy, you must be bursting for it and I didn't know. Have they neglected you, or is your Mamma afraid of doing too much?"

"Yes, Gertie, you love, they won't give me a chance, the key is turned in the lock every night so I can't enter her room except when she thinks proper. Let me have it quick!" as to keep up the deception I slipped off her lap, and trussing up her skirts, got between her lovely thighs and had my fingers in that luscious, golden-haired quim of hers. The touch was electric; she guided my rampant member into the haven of bliss, and being both of us just mad for a fuck, a very few strokes drew the juice of love in profusion, and she lay palpitating beneath me on the seat, her glorious cunt nipping and squeezing my prick most deliciously, as it retained its stiffness within her.

Another round followed, which we enjoyed more leisurely, and when I withdrew my limp tool she took it in her mouth, sucking it clean, then permitting me to do the same for her, said with a laugh: "That saves soiling one's handkerchief, besides it is so nice to know we love one another like that. You dear Perce, no more now, or you will feel too exhausted; what shall we talk about?"

"Auntie, it is a funny thing, but last night I had a dream and saw you and Thompson, the groom (George), meet a gentleman on horseback: such a handsome fellow—and you all went into a wood, tied up the three horses, and laid on the grass; you kissed the gentleman, and taking out his cock, said what a splendid affair it was, calling Thompson's attention to it; but the gentleman, who you called Charlie, laughingly declared he was sure Thompson had a grander one, whispering something in your ear, at which you blushed crimson, but exclaimed: 'I'll bet you, and pay forfeit if I lose.'"

74

"Done, but what shall be the stakes, if Thompson's is not the biggest, I will submit to a dozen good strokes from a birch switch cut from those bushes over there; but if I win you will have to take the dozen strokes on your own pretty bum. Is that agreed?"

Thompson was blushing to the roots of his hair: "Oh, don't make me the subject of the bet; you shan't look at mine."

"Oh, won't we, my boy?" Charlie said, suddenly seizing the groom by the leg, and bringing him down on the grass: "Now, help me, Gertie, we will soon look for ourselves."

Thompson did not resist very desperately, so as Charlie kept him down, my aunt Gertie's nimble fingers soon unfastened the fly of his trousers and fished out his tool, which was in a spending state, having emitted its thick creamy sperm all over his belly.

"Oh, my, Charlie, but it is a grand one though, and you win. Oh, how funny handling such a fine stiff affair makes me feel; I quiver all over."

"Ride on it then, you little bitch, and see if my switch does not make you dance well on it; you shall bound up and down till you have sucked every drop out of him."

The groom was passive in your hands, laying quiet enough, as Charlie made you straddle over him, and settle yourself down on his big upstanding prick, till it was all out of sight in your cunt. "Now ride him well, Gertie, or you will be made to move yourself," and he stepped away to cut his switch, a couple of minutes only sufficing him to make a handy tickler of long thin sprigs of birch.

You had been slowly riding up and down, evidently enjoying the slow motions as you rose and fell on the groom's splendid poker; your skirts were well tucked up over your hips so I could see the seething sperm oozing out at every down stroke you gave. Then Charlie came back and began lightly tickling your buttocks with his birch twigs, presently giving one or two smart little cuts which made you wince. "Now, Thompson hold tight round her waist, and buck up well to her, never mind how she squeaks, it will make a fine game for you; see if you don't enjoy it. You never had such a fuck before in your life, I'll bet."

His twigs now cut finely into your bum at each stroke, making long red marks, and a deep rosy tint all over each cheek of your buttocks; Oh, it was a sight, as Charlie went on faster and harder, you winced, sighed: "Oh, oh, oh, don't be cruel," and cried till the tears streamed down your face, but at length the spasm of pleasure seemed to make you oblivious to every other sensation as the groom appeared to meet you with a flood of his love juice, and you lay exhausted on the top of him, but only for a few moments, as Charlie was so madly randy he turned you over off the groom, and was into you himself, quicker than I can tell, whilst Thompson, quite pumped out, sat up and enjoyed the scene—just as I awoke to find it all a dream, and my own cock pumping up the semen all over my night shirt.

"How curious I should dream that, Auntie, don't you think so; did you ever have two cocks to play with at once like that? It must be a delicious idea."

"I believe Thompson has a grand prick," I continued. "You must have noticed the fine bunch he shows in his trousers."

"I've noticed it, but Perce, how your brain must be full of such things to dream that," she replied, fencing my question.

"Yes, and I fancy you must have had a taster of it some time or other, as I know you always take your enema for a ride with you."

This rather startled her, her face crimsoning all over. "Oh, you wicked boy; you have fucked little Patty, she only could have told you that."

"Well, Auntie, confidence for confidence is only fair; we are to have a fine spree with George, who you know is her brother, in the stable on Sunday morning, when all the others are gone to Church. Would you like to be in it? but don't let Pat know, it will be a fine surprise when she sees you with me; and how would you like two pricks in you at once—back and front?—it would be awfully grand, don't you think, my darling Auntie?"

"What a boy you are, Perce, to go on like that, why you must think I am well up in every kind of lubricity; it has never been my experience, much as I should like to see it. No doubt you and George have served poor Pat in that way. At any rate, whatever she has learnt from you lately, I have noticed how sprightly she looks—girls are always like that when they have once tasted the forbidden fruit. Did you take her maidenhead?"

"Yes, and Mary's too. Haven't I been lucky, Auntie, and how I should have liked to have been the first into you. Oh, it must have been a treat to the fellow who had it. Do you know it makes me feel an old hand at the game now? I don't mean to lose any chances, and will fuck every girl I come across, if I can only get over her."

"You are worse and worse every day, and how sly you have been. Anyhow I did get you first, and it was me who opened your eyes; to think of it makes me spend, does it affect my boy like that?" she asked, noticing the rampant state I was in. "Well just another, as we can't help ourselves."

This was a rare rock-off, the seat being just a convenient height; so standing between her legs, I shoved into her lovely cunt, taking her beautiful legs under my arms, and we could manage to kiss and suck each other's mouths at the same time, which made a delicious combination. "Don't hurry, make it last, my darling love of a boy."

Even gently fucking was too much for us, excited as we were. I could feel my crisis coming on, so to prolong my own pleasure (for I knew she

77

could keep on spending and coming continually) I withdrew and, falling on my knees, sucked and tongued that delicious cunt of hers, almost devouring the clitoris, which I sucked as hard as I could, getting it all between my lips and tongue, which rolled round it. Then to add to her erotic agony, my fingers frigged the tight bum-hole as the sperm from above trickled over it.

"Ah, oh, you darling love! I shall die if you work me up like that. Oh, shove your love of a prick up where your fingers are, it will be splendid just now."

Stiffer than ever, I plunged in, but not too fast. However, the insertion was speedily effected, and the contractions of that tightfitting anus delighted me beyond expression, so that, impossible to restrain myself, the boiling spunk shot right up to her bowels, as she screamed in the acme of her delight: "Oh, oh, ah-r-r-re! How divine! Lovely isn't the word to describe such rapturous sensations. Don't withdraw, you dear, your prick is stiffer than ever, as I feel it throbbing and swelling inside me. Go on, go on, for all you are worth, it is so well oiled you can't hurt or stretch me too much;" and I found she had one of her hands frigging herself in front doing everything possible to increase our delirium. On we went, till I again pumped my very life up to her vitals, and lay over her quite exhausted whilst my champion seemed to swell still more inside its burning hot sheath, and when at length I withdrew, is was with quite an audible plop I like a tight cork being drawn.

We parted with mutual caresses, and she promised to join our Sunday party.

Meanwhile George and I added sundry things to make our meeting more comfortable, especially in the way of wine and biscuits, &c.

My plan was for my auntie Gert to surprise us in the midst of a salacious scene, so was early at the stable, and George communicated the fact that the little mare was just come on, and we agreed to turn her into the stallion's stall to excite Patty, who arrived a few minutes after me—all blushes, especially when I joked her about looking so well, and that the last double spree had evidently done her a world of good to judge by the way her eyes sparkled.

"Oh, don't chaff me like that. Mr. Percy, it makes me fancy I can feel it even now, you almost split my poor bottom."

"Nonsense, you mean you would just like to feel it again, Pat. Now, haven't you dreamt about it every night?"

This made her blush more than ever, and I could see it was a good guess.

Jerry, the stallion pony, appeared in a very excited state.

Said George: "He's always like that when he can sniff Jenny. Shall I turn her in with him?"

"Yes, do George," said Pat: "it must be funny to see how they do it."

"Well, it's only fair," I replied, "the pony saw our spree the other day, so let her in, my boy, to please Pat and make her want a bit herself."

The little stallion greeted his mate with a very wild whinney, and his thick, black, india-rubber looking affair shot out in excitement as he wanted to mount her in an instant. I kept my eyes on Pat, whose blushing face only too plainly indicated how the scene affected her.

George held the mare's head, as Jerry mounted on her rump, but the stallion's penis quite failed to find the exact place of entrance, pushing and pushing without avail. "You must help him," said George, or he'll never get in.

"Come on, Pat," I cried, "you take hold of it and point it right for him, I'll help you, pushing her forward, it's nothing to mind doing." Her trembling fingers grasped the shiny black looking tool, and pointed it to the vulva of the little mare, who stood with her hind legs planted firmly apart, without whisking her tail; my fingers opened the slit a little, the stallion snorted, and with one plunge got in the full length of his affair, seeming to shoot his sperm at the same moment; in fact, Patty declared she quite felt the spasm shoot through the thing, which swelled and stiffened as it throbbed, the mixed emissions of the animal squirting all down the mare's thighs, as the stallion repeated his strokes; but it was quickly over, he withdrew at once and his tool hung down dripping and slimy, whilst we could see the mare's cunt opening a little and quivering from the recent excitement; both seemed satisfied, and Jenny was put back into her box at once, Patty remarking:

"What a silly business, it is so soon over, I should want it again and again: it's made me so randy for a fuck. Do have me, some one at once." She had pulled up her skirts and was straddling over one end of the stool, frigging herself, so to oblige Patty, I quickly pushed her backwards, and got into her longing slit. The grind did not last long, both being so hot for it, so it came off in a very few strokes.

"Now," said I, drawing out, "that was only just to steady ourselves. We don't wish to be like animals, but enjoy the game properly; these short rapid fucks give very little pleasure or satisfaction, the sensations are much too transient."

"Hey! this is the game, is it? I've been watching your goings on through that hole," said Aunt Gert, bursting in upon us. "You thought everyone had gone to church, did you? and you, Patty Thompson, behaving like that, when I always considered you such a quiet, virtuous girl. Oh, fie! no wonder men think all girls are alike," in her pretended indignation. "Now, what am I to do? Pretty goings on for your Mamma to know of, Percy. I shall take and give you a good sound thrashing, now I am so thoroughly roused, and your wicked bottom shall smart, I can promise you. After that, I will settle what is to be done with that wretched brother and sister," as gripping my arm she tried to drag me away with her.

80

"No, no, you don't, I'm not taking any, Aunt Gert, beside you might hurt. Here you, George and Pat, just help me, and we'll serve her out for spying on us—then, perhaps she won't be fast to tell tales."

Patty had been in an awful state of fright, but now helped George and me so drag Gertie forward, shutting the stable door, which we securely bolted.

"Ah, no, how dare you?" she screamed, well knowing no one could hear the row. "Let me go: you shan't, you shan't, you little beast, Percy!" as I tried to pull up her skirts: but we got her down on the straw, and soon exposed all her private affairs in spite of struggles and kicks, then turning her over on her face, they held her firmly, whilst I gave her lovely plumb buttocks such a slapping that she screamed under it, begging to be let go, promising to do anything and keep our secret.

"Well, then, let George fuck you, I want to look on, and frig Patty to make her do all the ponies do."

Placing George on the stool, Patty made him lay on his back, then opening his trousers, presented his lordly prick to our view. "Now, Auntie, that's your penance, to ride a cock-horse on as fine an instrument as you could wish for. Just straddle across him, and he will hold your waist tight enough, so you can't fall off."

Although pretending to be so very indignant, she did not give me much trouble to adjust her, not liking the savage pinches I gave her firm bottom, until I had had the satisfaction of seeing George's splendid affair right up her, till the hair on their parts mingled. "Now, move yourself, Auntie," I called out, giving the beautiful bottom a tremendous slap with my hand, just as she had drawn what I knew to be a deep sigh of satisfaction at feeling that grand prick swelling and filling her vagina to its utmost capacity. Her buttocks fairly jerked up under the impact of my hand, and as she came down again on his delighted pego, George clasped her round the waist so that she lay along on him, and their lips would meet. My fingers busily tickled alternately his balls, or played round the clinging lips of her quim, as the spendings began to ooze out in profusion each time the prick went home, enabling me to plentifully lubricate her little wrinkled nether hole, which I contemplated presently to attack, only waiting till their emotions should make her regardless of what I might be about. George heaved up beneath her, to meet every grasp of her greedy cunt, sinking down on him, as if it would eat such a delicious morsel, the uttermost bit of which it seemed eager to swallow.

With lips glued together they swived and squealed in ecstasy. Patty was beside herself at the sight of it, and seizing hold of my prick wanted to suck it, which I did permit for a moment or two, for the sake of the lubrication: then whispering the dear girl what I wanted, she pointed its glistening head to Gertie's fundament, as I seized hold of my aunt's hips and pushed gently. Then, as the head got in, I felt the voluptuous contractions of the small aperture. I was mad to get in and feel my prick rubbing against that of George, with only a thin membrane between them. Only those who have experienced this double enjoyment can realize the delicate and intoxicating sensations of such a moment.

"My God! Oh, Perce! You kill me with pleasure—this beats anything I ever imagined. Oh, heavens, my very life will be drawn out of me: you make me spend so, it thrills all up my spine to my brain. Ah, oh, I'm done!" as she collapsed into a state of momentary obliviousness.

Patty had been sitting on a sack of chaff, as she handled my balls or postillioned me behind and covered my bottom with hottest kisses. Seeing the climax was over with Gertie she pulled me away, saying. "Put it into me quick, it must be lovely like that, all slimy and so awfully stiff. You don't know how I do want my turn, you dear." Excited as I was, another cunt to finish in was just the thing for me, so I rolled on top of the amorous girl, and in no time was ranging up and down her luscious affair, to the great gratification of such a salacious nature. The stiffness was almost painfully nice to me, and I lasted so well that Patty was fairly fucked out, as well as my aunt, at the end of our encounter.

82

When we came to ourselves, it was only to find Gertie kissing and sucking George's member, which was again ready for action, so I placed Patty's well-buttered affair over him for a ride, and by Gertie's help soon was able to put in behind and complete the girl's happiness, which I knew she was longing for.

After this we refreshed and adjusted ourselves, and thus finished Sunday's matinee.

Now having my darling mother, Auntie Gert, Mary, and Patty at my disposal in the house, the precocious lubricity of my nature had full swing for a time, and to reiterate the scenes of lust I took part in would be too tedious.

Patty alone of that female quartette was a scorcher who would capture me at every possible safe opportunity, and her warm kisses on my lips always had such a magnetic influence on me they effected immediately a rise below.

However, wishing for a change from such a surfeit of poking, gamahuching, &c, my thoughts turned to Phoebe and her little girls, so calling at the cottage one fine afternoon, to my surprise the door was opened by a beautiful girl of about fourteen, neatly dressed in a bright cotton frock, just short enough to display the contour of her finely shaped legs and ankles, with a mass of blue-black hair hanging over her shoulders and down her back, so I should think she might have sat on it. She was a vision of delight, and at a glance I recognised she must be a sister to Phoebe.

"Oh, don't mind me. I see your were doing up your hair. You must be Phoebe's sister—is she out?"

"Yes, sir," she replied, blushing deeply: "and are you Mr. Percy from the hall, she and the girls so often speak about? They have all gone to market, but will be back to tea."

"I am sorry, because I came on purpose to enquire how she was. You know about a fortnight ago she did not seem at all right, so I have brought her a bottle of wine. I must rest myself a bit; it has been a tiring walk, and I always make myself at home here," as I walked in without being invited.

She placed a chair for me, then saying she would just tie up her hair, stepped into the back bedroom, leaving the door slightly ajar.

"Excuse me," I said, following her: "but may I wash my hands. You need not mind me, go on with your hair, but it can't look better than it does now."

Merely dipping my hands in the water she poured out for me, taking the towel, I remarked. "Do just leave it as it is. I shall soon be gone, but must have a kiss first," then dropping the towel. "Phoebe has always kissed me ever since I can remember, so why shouldn't you, my dear?" placing an arm round her waist.

"Oh, no, I can't. You never saw me before; I shall run into the garden unless you behave yourself, Mr. Percy," trying to get away from me, but I held her too fast. "Now don't be cross. Kissing is so nice, and you must just give me one, just one, and I'll let you go," overcoming her slight resistance and smothering that crimson face with kisses. "Now do, or I shall go on kissing you, dear, it's more than I can help. You are so nice."

"Well then, only a little one," she lisped, just touching my cheek with her lips.

"Ah, no, that isn't a good one. Why I could kiss you all over, if you had no clothes on," as one of my hands was slipped inside the bosom of her dress, having slyly unfastened one or two hooks.

"No, no? You shan't, Mr. Percy. What should I do if Phoebe was to come in?"

"But she will be two hours yet, you little goose; how can a kiss or a touch hurt you?"

84

Her lips met mine, and I took a long, luscious kiss, almost sucking her breath away, and my hand was in possession of one of the small firm globes of her bosom, still more increasing her confusion, as I rubbed and played with the rosy nipples and moved my hand from one to the other little strawberry tips. This could not go on in a standing posture, so I pushed her against the edge of the bed—kissing and groping till she seemed quite oblivious of what was happening to her, laying back on the coverlet in a dazed kind of state—and, devil that I was, it took no time to part her beautiful legs, which I found protected by prettily frilled drawers, which still hid the charms of her person from my groping fingers. I wanted to look, but was afraid to withdraw my kissing from her lips, for fear she might recover herself and resist my encroachments below.

My ardent prick stood like a bar of ivory, impatient for a breach to be opened for his advance to the assault of her tender virginity. Nervously my fingers pulled at the impeding linen, till they found a small opening and could touch the downy furniture of her mount, and finding the entrance to Love's Palace of Pleasure, slowly parted the velvety lips of her maiden slit. Then gently tickling the sensitive clitty, that source of every girl's delight, made her sigh out: "Ah, oh! how nice, Mr. Percy! don't hurt me, will you—there's a dear!" as her bum squirmed under the novel sensations my touches had roused and the warmth of her kisses now plainly gave her away.

Writing this, as I do after many years of varied experiences, I may remark that mere verbal appeals to any girl's sensibility have very little influence in inducing them to yield to salacious suggestions—it is the warmth of contact and lascivious touches which undo them—a few hot kisses, pressure on the bosom, and groping their love slit (even if you have to use considerable force) which make them ready to consent. Their blood gets fired in a moment, and resist as they may, they want it and cannot help themselves; then once done, it is a very rare exception if there is not some little feeling of love towards even a ravisher; he must be a brute who provokes any feelings of aversion.

"Look here, darling, you make me love you so; I'll give you five golden sovereigns I have in my purse, only let me kiss your naked body; it's no harm, no one can see us, and so awfully jolly. Only think, all that money for your own little self, to buy nice things with, and do as you like."

"You undress me then, I'm too ashamed to do it, Percy," she said in a low voice. "Oh! you do make me feel so funny all over!"

Giving her an extra luscious kiss, I attacked hooks, buttons, and strings, till in a jiffy she had nothing but her stockings left to adorn her figure, covering her face with her hands to hide her shame at such exposure.

Giving her no time for reflection, but taking advantage of such a state of abandon, my lips and tongue ranged all over her bosom and belly, leaving the most secret casket of all for a last bonne bouche, and as my tongue titillated her, beginning down at the abdomen and moving slowly till it revelled under her hairless arm-pit. She fairly quivered under the intensity of the feelings aroused: "Ah! Oh! Oh! How delicious that was, it thrills me all over, Percy, do that again with your tongue all the way up." Once more the electricity of my tongue sent vibrations of a new and sensuous pleasure through every nerve and vein of her body. She seemed beside herself, exclaiming: "Let me bite you, and kiss you, my darling. Ah, you have all your clothes still on! I want to feel your soft flesh as well as your touches, it would double the pleasure."

"Do you think so, my love? I'll soon be like you and let you do as you wish with me, as long as I can press your lovely person in my arms," stripping myself as quickly as I could tear off the obstructing apparel, then, naked as Adam, I knelt between her widely opened legs and imprinted a kiss on the pinky lips of her tight looking little cunny, as they just peeped out between the downy chevelure, forcing my tongue in between them till it found that hypersensitive little button of love. This so electrified her that she almost bounded off the bed; again and again my tongue played around it, as she seemed dying with delight, making her scream out: "Oh, you love? Oh, my darling! What is it I feel thrilling me through and through. Ah, what is it? What is going to happen? I feel something coming! Oh! oh! oh! I'm done!" as she gave down a flood of maiden spend, thick and glutinous, all over my lips, as I eagerly sucked every pearly drop.

Laying in a sort of dazed ecstasy, now was my chance, so standing up and throwing my naked body over her, my affair was with its ruby head touching the lips of her cunt.

We kissed each other ardently, as her arms clasped round my body. "Oh, how lovely, to feel your flesh like this, you are all mine just now, Percy; but what is that I feel trying to push into me down there?"

"Feel for yourself, dearest, it is the ladies' darling; they call it my prick, or my cock, and love to have it go in there. Put your hand on it, dear, and your happiness will soon be complete, if you just open those little lips of yours and rub the head against the little spot my tongue tickled so nicely: let me help you."

One of my hands directed hers, and placed it on my prick, the small soft fingers grasped round it, giving me such a thrill that I gave a hard push, jamming the head just a little within the entrance to her virginity, "Oh, oh! You hurt me, Percy! Don't be so rough again."

"You pet; it's made to go in there, then you'll be a real woman, and know what love is: bear it for a moment, I must have you now."

A natural instinct seemed to direct her motions, for just then giving a deep sigh, she heaved up to meet, and I gained another inch, making her give quite a little scream of pain. Push, push, push, I went on drawing a sharp cry of agony at each advance. Presently something snapped and gave way before my impetuous charge, the victory was won, but not without some loss of blood, as I found when having shot a stream of my healing balsam into her lacerated parts, I was able to withdraw for a wash, whilst she lay in a dazed kind of lost state, till having purified myself, I applied a wet handkerchief to wipe and soothe her still, burning

87

parts. "Oh, how nice of you to think of me like that," she said, opening her eyes, looking me all over. "And is that the thing that has hurt me so?" as she pointed to my now limp John Thomas. "Why it felt like a warm bar of iron forcing itself into me."

Leaning over her I kissed repeatedly her impudent looking titties, as they stood up to invite my lips, and as I did so, felt one of her hands steal down to the ravisher of her virginity.

"La, how soft it is now!" she whispered. "Will it get hard again soon?"

"Keep hold, and see, my darling: do you want it put in again?"

How my question made her blush, as she replied, "But not if I am to be hurt as much the next time; still I fancy it must be nice when there is no pain in getting in. Ah! how it's swelling in my hand. Perhaps if you put it there before it is too big, I could bear it better, do just try, Percy, my love."

"Point it there yourself, pet, and I will be as gentle as possible," I said, getting between her legs, her hand retaining its hold on my fast stiffening champion, which I slowly pressed forward as she directed it: her face twitched as she evidently felt a trifle sore, but her own lubricity so oiled the tight passage, I was soon in to the roots of my hair, which rubbed against her downy little door mat.

"There, it's all in again; did I hurt you much?" as she squirmed her body closer to me, pressing me tightly in her arms.

"Only a wee bit, Percy, dear; you were so gentle with me; the first time you seemed to rush at me so furiously, but just now it slipped in nicely, and I feel it there swelling bigger and bigger every moment; my poor little thing is quite stretched to hold it, you actually seem part of myself."

"Yes, darling, and now there is no pain, you will presently feel as if my very soul was flowing into you," I replied, beginning the gentle in and out motion, slowly withdrawing, then again penetrating to the uttermost extent of her capacity. "That is lovely! Ah, Percy, my dear, you make me feel delights I never had an idea of before this. Oh, oh, it's coming again! I'm flowing. Push, push, I want every bit of it. Oh, faster!" as she plunged about and bucked up at every stroke.

"Darling, I'm coming too. There, there, how do you like my spunk shooting up into you?"

"Oh, my pet, my love, it drives me wild! No other pleasure can be like it!" kissing my lips, face, and neck in her ecstasy, till her teeth gave me a sharp love bite.

We lay swimming in love juice, my prick swelling and throbbing inside her deliciously tight sheath, which treated it to such contractions and lascivious nippings I thought I should never be able to withdraw, as her cunt held on to my prick as if would never lose hold of such a treasure.

However, the sweetest of fucks must have an end, so at length I persuaded her to get up and dress, for fear Phoebe and the girls might come home a little too soon.

"And when shall we see each other again, pet?" I said, kissing her flushed face, "as I must go home now."

"I'm only here till to-morrow morning. If you had but come three or four days ago; now I must go back to my place to-morrow. I'm only a nursemaid you know, in London, and may not have a chance to see you for ever so long: and to think how I love you now!" she said, kissing me with tears in her eyes.

"And I don't even know your name, darling, yet. What is it?" repaying kiss for kiss.

"It's Kitty Sawyer; and won't you write to me Percy, at Mrs. Blanks,

The Chestnuts, Westbourne Grove, London? Write it down, there's a dear."

"Kitty, of course, I will, and what's more whenever I'm in London will be sure to meet you. You promise to get out, won't you?"

"Yes, I'd see you, Percy, if I had to lose my place for it. What a pity I can't be at the Hall, but there's no baby there."

Thus we parted with mutual endearments, as I thought it best to defer seeing Phoebe and her girls until another day, and will continue that part of my romance in another volume to be written very shortly.

Note from the Editor.

Odin's Library Classics strives to bring you unedited and unabridged works of classical literature. As such this is the complete and unabridged version of the original. The English language has evolved since the writing and some of the words appear in their original form, or at least the form most commonly used at the time. This is done to protect the original intent of the author. If at any time you are unsure of the meaning of the original meaning of a word, please do your research on that word. It is important to preserve the history of the English language.

Taylor Anderson

Made in the USA
Middletown, DE
21 May 2021